SING ME A LOVE SONG

A LIGHT & LOVE SWEET ROMANCE

LEE STRAUSS

COPYRIGHT

Originally published as part of The Minstrel Series/The Guitar Girls as Lee Strauss/Hope Franke Strauss.

TWO DAYS AGO

OPEN MIC NIGHT at the Blue Note Pub.

Katja signed her name on the performer's list and hoped she'd be called to play. If the manager liked her he might let her book a whole night. It happened sometimes. Not only could she make a hundred euros, but her name would also be on the posters.

Katja Stoltz

Money and fame. She needed both.

The bar wasn't huge. It had a low, wood-beamed ceiling with wooden floors and long tables that were already occupied, making the space feel even smaller. She shuffled past the other musicians and music lovers, holding her guitar case close to her chest. Her eyes darted around the room, searching for a place to sit.

A guy with brown hair shaved short watched her. She'd seen him before, though they'd never spoken, just the kindred nod that happened between musicians as they acknowledged each other's guitar. He had a peacock tattoo that stretched across his strumming arm, which was draped over a thin girl with spiky blond hair. The guy waved Katja over, shoving down on the bench to make room. Katja pushed loose strands of hair behind her ear and took the offered seat. She flashed him a bright, sincere smile. "Thanks."

"It's cool. You're playing tonight?" he asked loudly to cut through the din of conversation and the music pumping in through the speakers hanging from the corners of the room.

"I hope so. You?"

The guy shrugged. "Maybe. Rock's more my thing, but acoustic's cool, too. I'm Sebastian. This is my girlfriend, Yvonne."

Yvonne forced a smile but didn't make eye contact. Sebastian introduced the rest of the table, but their names disappeared into the clatter of the room.

As each musician was called, Katja's stomach spun tighter. The artists were good and she applauded appreciatively with the rest of the crowd after each performer.

The waiter brought drinks to their table and asked Katja if she'd like to order. She'd love to, but she shook her head no. She couldn't even spare ten cents.

"It's on me," Sebastian said, surprising her. "Bring her a beer."

Yvonne glared at him. Sebastian laughed and squeezed her shoulders. "Baby, it's okay. The chick's gotta be thirsty, and she's singing tonight."

Katja mouthed thank you. She *was* thirsty. She wanted to impress Herr Leduc, the manager, and it would be much harder to do that with a dry throat. He'd been very friendly when she first introduced herself a few weeks ago, welcoming her to his pub with exuberant German laced with a thick French accent.

Finally, Katja's name was called. She made her way through the crowd, careful not to bang into anyone with her guitar. The lights were bright on the stage, momentarily blinding her. She strapped her guitar over her shoulder and scanned the crowd.

She gulped, thinking belatedly that maybe it wasn't a great idea to be doing her newest song.

Her eyes landed on Sebastian and he lifted his beer to her before taking a long drink.

"Hello, everyone," she said while tuning the bottom string of her guitar. "I'm Katja Stoltz and this is a new song."

She plucked the notes with a happy, mid-paced beat. The music didn't match the words. She'd written it that way on purpose, to get the listeners' attention. She opened her mouth and her smooth, folk voice sang out.

Close your eyes
Try not to speak
Forget the hours of your struggling
Try to fix the trouble
And pieces of your broken mind

The streets that you are traveling on
They lead you far away from home
And you don't know where you're going to
And your dreams
They all turned
A somber blue
This burden on your shoulders
Is too heavy for you to carry
And the well
That you're drinking from
Is a well from a dying generation

Think back to when you were a child

And your heart was free and you were alive
And the wind
And the rain
Washed all your fears away

She ended the song with a final strum and the applause rang through the house. She couldn't stop the sappy smile that spread across her face. She left the stage and was accosted by a group sitting at a nearby table.

"That was awesome."

"Love your voice!"

"Do you have CDs?"

She thanked them and produced a short stack of CDs. She sold four. This was *great*! She bounced happily on the tips of her toes. Now she could pay her rent *and* buy a new set of strings.

She felt a poke on the shoulder and turned around to see Sebastian grinning down at her.

"You rocked it, Katja. You have crazy songwriting skills."

She couldn't help but giggle. This was why she loved writing and performing. There was no high like it.

"Do you wanna hang out sometime, maybe write together?"

Katja couldn't keep the surprise from bubbling over. "That would be great." She'd love to try writing with another songwriter. Then she caught Yvonne glaring at them from where she'd remained seated at their table. "But, I don't think she's…."

Sebastian glanced over his shoulder and waved at his girlfriend. "Don't worry about her. She knows she's the only one for me."

How nice for Yvonne to have someone so dedicated to her. Sebastian obviously loved her and Katja hoped she appreciated it. She would love to know what it felt like to have someone love her fully without conditions.

And she would. She was certain. Someday.

YESTERDAY

THE HOT WATER tank in Irma and Martina's flat was the size of a backpack.

Katja squirmed under the cooling water as she rinsed the last of the shampoo from her hair. The stall was barely big enough to turn around in, and she'd learned to watch her elbows, not to accidentally knock into the tap and either scald herself or dose her bare body with ice water. Every shower was a race to finish before the hot water disappeared.

It occurred to her that this was why her roommates both kept their hair short. Maybe she should take the scissors to hers, too. She winced at the thought. Her long, golden locks were her trademark. She'd just have to struggle through the hair-washing trauma.

The clothes she'd washed in the sink the day before still hadn't dried, so she was forced to wear her red gypsy skirt and grey blouse for the second day in a row.

She cleaned up her things and headed to the kitchen for a coffee. Now that she had a little extra cash, she could buy the next bag of beans, and she wouldn't have to feel guilty about drinking her roommates' coffee.

Katja yawned. She scanned the flat as she waited for the coffee to brew. Irma and Martina had thrown a party the night before. Empty beer bottles and full ashtrays littered the room. The smell of smoke lingered in the air, and if it weren't so cold outside, Katja would've opened a window. At least they couldn't blame her for the messy state of affairs this time.

Their guests hadn't left until the early morning hours, long after Katja had returned from her gig. Times like that she really wished she had her own place. As it was she had to wait for space to open up on the sofa, and eventually she nodded off even though some strange guy stubbornly refused to leave his spot at the other end.

It was noon before anyone started waking up. Katja had a horrible kink in her neck and a growing headache. Outside the church bells rang, which didn't really help.

Irma sauntered into the room. Her short, black hair stood up in all directions, and dark puffy circles marred the skin under her eyes. She poured a cup of coffee and sipped it like it would save her life. She drank half of it before noticing Katja sitting there.

"Oh, hey. I heard you rocked the house last night." She slid into a chair opposite Katja.

"Yeah, it was fun," Katja said. She'd replayed her performance and the small crowd's response in her head a million times. The thrill of having her talent recognized still energized her. "Herr Leduc offered me a night of my own."

Irma arched a dark eyebrow. "Really?"

It annoyed her that Irma didn't even try to hide her surprise, like she didn't think Kaja had it in her.

"Yeah, really."

Irma *harrumphed* and took another sip.

"I have the rent," Katja announced. She moved confidently to the living room, rested on the sofa and heaved her duffle bag onto her lap. She dug through her things, lifting rumpled shirts and dirty jeans, scraping her nails along the bottom, fingers searching. Her heart sped up. Where was her wallet? She knew she'd put it in here last night when she got home. Icy apprehension filled her chest. She dumped the contents of her bag on the sofa.

No wallet. *No, no no!*

"It's gone," she muttered. A prickly dread washed over her and her joints felt weak. "Someone stole my wallet."

"Are you sure?"

Katja frantically sorted through everything again. "Yes, it's gone."

"That sucks," Irma said. "But you got that gig coming up at the Blue Note, right?"

"That's not until next month." Katja's eyes grew glassy and she swallowed the lump in her throat. She felt so violated. So disempowered. Now she couldn't pay her portion of the rent. "What am I going to do?"

Irma cocked a brow. "There are other ways to make good money in one night."

Katja frowned. "How?"

Irma tilted her head. "You are very naïve, aren't you? I'm not one to give out easy compliments, but you do have great legs. Get rid of that granny dress and show them off."

TODAY

Katja stood in one of the cutaways on the old bridge over the River Elbe that joined the *Altstadt* with the *Neustadt*, the old city with the new.

She shivered despite her winter jacket and the scarf wrapped around her neck and strummed her guitar with fingerless gloves. The limestone dome of the *Frauenkirche*—the Church of our Lady—peaked out over the city's ancient, baroque skyline. Like all the buildings in the historic center, it had been completely demolished during the Second World War. The entire city was rebuilt to look much like it had before it was destroyed. In essence, the old town was now the new one, and the new town the old one.

It was majestic and awe-inspiring to look upon.

Most days.

Katja's guitar case lay open at her feet. She'd thrown in the few cents she'd found under the sofa cushions, hoping to lure other donations.

The cold wind kept people hunched over and moving at a fast pace across the bridge, most with chins tucked down and hands shoved into deep pockets. No one took the time to stop and listen, much less drop money in her case.

Go home.

No! That would mean admitting failure. It would prove

that Horst was right about her. She was nothing but a thankless leach.

He was no better. A low-class scumbag. Why should she care what he thought?

Besides, it wasn't like her mother had thrown her out. She probably wouldn't even notice if Katja quietly moved back in. She could go back to university, get a diploma or a degree, something that would land her a real job.

But going back would mean she gave up on her dreams, that she'd be trapped in a lower middle-class life in Berlin. Horst would definitely mock her—and worse. Bile burned up the back of her throat at the thought of him touching her again. No, she couldn't go back.

She was talented and she knew it. It was just a matter of time. She couldn't give up.

Katja closed her eyes and started another song. She heard the clank of coins falling into her case. She looked up to see the old woman who'd dropped the money and thanked her with a quick nod.

By mid-afternoon her fingers were frozen stiff and she had to go to the bathroom. A glance at the coinage told her that she hadn't made near enough to cover the rent. She sighed heavily and packed up. The ten-minute walk back to her flat felt much, much longer.

Katja stared at the two tiers of fabric she'd ripped off her gypsy skirt lying on the floor like blood that had seeped from her own body. She breathed into her hands, forcing her lungs to expand and deflate at a proper rate, willing her heart to slow.

She didn't want to do this, but she didn't have a choice. It was too cold to sleep outside and even if she survived one night, there was always the next and the next. Spring weather was late coming to Saxony this year.

It wasn't like she didn't know what to expect. She had her first boyfriend at sixteen. Niklas Reinhardt. She'd crushed on him for a whole year prior to the outdoor party where he finally noticed her. They hooked up that night, and he'd clung to her for the next two years. He'd told her that everyone was doing it and it was expected that a girl-friend give it up for her guy. He was drunk the first time they did it, and it had hurt, but it wasn't completely awful.

She didn't know why she stayed with him as long as she did. He was good looking in a geeky, teenage-boy way, but she never loved him. He worked well as a buffer to keep all the other hormonal boys away, though. Dealing with one was enough trouble.

Irma lent her a pair of black high-heel shoes and offered advice. "You'll be freezing but you can't act like it. If you have to wear that jacket, at least leave it open. Mess your hair up and wear this." She handed Katja a tube of bright red lipstick.

Katja applied it with a trembling hand, feeling flustered as her roommate watched her put it on.

Once outside, Katja wasn't sure where to go.

She thought staying in *Neustadt* was her best bet. During the day, the town was family friendly, with mothers and fathers pushing baby carriages and holding small hands. Alongside the families, the elderly strolled slowly, and the punks walked their dogs and carried boom boxes. Every wall was either tagged or papered with posters

11

announcing the latest band or event. The bohemian, grunge atmosphere of *Neustadt* called to artists and inspired unique shopping venues that attracted tourists from all over the world.

At night, it was a perpetual party place. Music blared from the clubs and bars. People roamed freely with open drinks, seemingly unaffected by the cold. There was laughing and shouting and stumbling over the cobblestones. The graffiti artists came out along with the pot smokers. It was a fun, happy place, where young and old partied together.

You could sell drugs, and you could sell sex.

Katja stood on a corner, propped a hand on her hip and presented a long leg covered with sheer, black hosiery. What was left of her red gypsy skirt ended snugly, high on her thigh. She resisted giving into full-on shivering, and pasted a big, phony smile on her face.

She could do this.

No, she couldn't. It was irresponsible and it was dangerous.

Her confidence faltered and she bit down on her lip ring to keep from bursting into an ugly cry.

Oh, God, what was she doing?

If she went back to Berlin…

Maybe she would call. It was a throwaway phone, the only kind she could afford and she was down to her last three minutes. If she called, it would be the last time. She was too cold to think it through and pressed the number on quick dial. She held the phone to her ear with frozen fingers and almost hung up, but a young voice answered after the third ring.

"Sibylle Bergmann,"

"Hi, Sibylle. It's Katja."

"Where are you?" Katja caught the tremble in her sister's voice. "When are you coming home?"

"I don't know. Is everything all right?"

When her sister didn't answer, Katja grew nervous. Her minutes were running out. "Is Mama there, Sibylle?"

Katja heard static and assumed her sister was fetching her mother. *Hurry*. But then she heard the one voice that made her blood curdle.

"Get your tight rear-end back here, brat!"

Katja disconnected the call and let out a low groan. A quick check on her time allotment showed eighteen seconds left. Not even worth keeping. She chucked the phone into the nearest trash bin.

Fine. This was her reality. She would deal with it. Whatever happened to her tonight could be no worse than if she went back and faced her step-father. And he wouldn't bother paying.

She took short, quick breaths to regain her composure, and then unzipped her jacket with stiff, red fingers. She forced another smile and turned to face the driver of a silver car that had slowed to a stop at the curb.

She tilted her hips and presented her legs, raking her long hair with frozen fingers.

The window rolled down and a man in a shirt and tie peered out.

"It's cold. Get in."

MICAH

Katja hesitated for a moment before opening the glossy, silver door and sliding into the passenger seat. It was a nice car. Really nice. An Audi. Katja wasn't a car connoisseur but she new Audis were expensive. It even smelled expensive. It had smooth, grey leather seats and an impressive digital console with all the bells and whistles. And it was warm. Heat even radiated from the seat underneath her, and that was all she could focus on for the first few minutes. She blew on her fingers.

She could feel the guy's eyes pouring over her. She glanced back, working to keep her expression friendly. She was surprised by his youthfulness. She'd expected to end up with someone much older, but this guy seemed close to her age. He wasn't bad-looking either. She could've done far worse. He had dark, curly hair that was cropped short, a slight shadow of a beard on his chin and jaw and deep-set, dark eyes. Under a black wool pea jacket he wore a dress shirt with a tie loosened around the collar and the top button undone.

His eyes were wide and glassy, and Katja thought maybe he was on something. He gripped the steering wheel tightly with both hands. He looked more freaked out than she was, and she wondered if maybe this was the first time he'd picked up a girl for pay.

"I'm Katja," she said, hoping to calm him. "What's your name?"

He swallowed and pulled out into traffic, staring hard at the road in front of him. "I'm Micah." He had a slight accent.

"Are you American?"

He glanced at her. "Half. My mother's American. My father is German."

"What part of America is she from?" Katja had never been outside of Germany and was fascinated by American culture. Especially the music scene.

He mumbled, "New York," like he really wasn't interested in talking to her about it. Of course, he wasn't. He thought she was a prostitute. She stared out the window and doodled on the condensation caused by her warm breath.

"Where are we going?" Katja finally asked. She assumed they were headed to a hotel room. Oh, no. Maybe she was supposed to have arranged a spot?

Micah spoke softly. "To my place."

Katja's heart skipped. Was it safe to go to a "client's" personal home? Was this guy some kind of serial killer? She just wanted to make rent, not end up in tomorrow's news.

Micah must've sensed her reluctance. "It's just… more comfortable there."

She heard herself say, "Yeah, sure. That's fine," but her flesh prickled with apprehension. What was this guy going to do to her? Tie her up? Beat her? She'd heard stories.

She gulped and stared blankly at the fogged-up window. This was a terrible mistake. But would jumping out of a moving car be any less dangerous?

Her eyes darted back to the driver. He didn't look like a killer, not that she knew what a killer looked like. The guy seemed to relax a little now that it was decided where they were going. Katja studied his profile. Though his jaw was tight and tense, he had nice eyes.

He couldn't be dangerous. She was just letting her imagination get away from her. And judging by the guy's car and clothes, he obviously could afford to pay her.

Katja's neck flushed at the thought of what she was about to do. Irma told her it wasn't so bad. Just close your eyes and think of something else, something pleasant. It'd be over before she knew it. Guys wanted what they wanted in a hurry.

Katja knew this to be true by unfortunate experience. It was part of the injustice in the world, a world especially cruel toward women. She wasn't the first to have to sell her body to survive and she wouldn't be the last.

She would close her eyes tightly and escape to somewhere else, far away in her mind. She'd think about her guitar and the latest song she was working on. She would imagine playing on a large stage under colorful lights in front of a paying crowd, a huge one that cheered for her when she finished performing. She'd have enough money for whatever she wanted. She would live in a nice, warm, cozy place. A *safe* place. She'd be respected and valued. She would never be hungry.

It would be okay.

HIS PLACE

His APARTMENT WAS *a lot* nicer than hers. He had matching furniture and a large flat-screen TV.

Katja stood in the middle of the living room unsure about what to do next. She removed her jacket and propped a hand on her hip, trying to look like a tempting vixen instead of the scared little girl she really was. She caught Micah's eye and removed her scarf slowly, staring at him with what she hoped were provocative eyes.

Instead of responding to her signals, Micah walked to the window that overlooked the river, shoved his hands in his pockets and stared out with his back to her. Why had he even bothered to stop for her anyway? He could easily have hired someone classier.

The silence was thick and awkward, and Katja thought maybe she should bolt. The door was right there, unlocked. Get away before any craziness started.

Micah turned slowly to face her. "Are you hungry?"

Katja blinked. Yeah, starving, but she wasn't here to eat. She forced a smile. "Maybe we should get started."

The corners of Micah's mouth twitched. "I'd rather not... on an empty stomach."

Fine. "Okay, sure. Let's eat."

Micah motioned for her to take a seat at the table, and

he proceeded to make a warm meal. Katja didn't know what to think. She sat straight-backed with her hands on her lap. Micah removed dishes from cupboards and drawers and food from the refrigerator. Soon the large, open apartment filled with the aroma of schnitzel and fried potatoes.

Her stomach growled.

Micah glanced at her a few times as he worked, but didn't comment.

"Can I set the table?" she asked. He pointed to a cupboard and she found the plates and glasses inside. She removed two of each and placed them on the table across from each other. She noticed the cutlery drawer from when Micah had removed a spoon, and took out forks and knives for each of them.

He dished out the meal, along with a salad that was already prepared in the fridge and opened a bottle of sparkling water. She smiled as he filled her glass, secretly wishing it was something stronger than water. She could really use a drink right about now.

Katja almost felt like she was dining at a restaurant. The only thing missing was a candle. "Smells great," she said.

He offered her a hint of a grin. *"Guten Appetit."*

Once she started eating, she found it hard to slow down. It had been forever since she'd eaten a meal like this. Micah watched her with a stoney expression, concern flashing in his eyes.

She smiled and made a joke of it. "My cooking is crap."

His expression didn't change and he remained silent. This guy is a piece of work, she thought. Zero personality.

She finished her meal, and then remembered why she

was there. Suddenly, she wished she hadn't eaten so much or so fast. She felt ill.

The silence was driving her crazy. Couldn't he at least turn on the TV or the stereo?

"So, what do you do, Micah?" she asked. Micah's eyes remained flat, and she wondered if she'd crossed a line by asking another personal question.

He finally answered, "I work at a bank."

Katja nodded as if that explained everything.

"How about you?" he countered. "When you're not doing... this?"

Katja sat back, unsure what she should divulge, if anything. She nibbled her lip ring. He answered her question. It was only fair that she answer his.

"I'm a musician." She feigned a laugh. "The pay's not that great."

Micah rose and carried his dirty dishes to the sink, rinsed them and loaded the dishwasher. Katja stood to help, placing her own dishes into the sink. The move caused her to stand close to his side, and she felt him stiffen.

If she knew what she was doing, she'd know how to make him relax. She'd also know how to get him to hand over the money. She honestly didn't know how to do either.

"I've never done this before," she admitted.

Micah stepped back, his eyes scanning her from head to toe. He surprised her by saying, "I'm glad."

He disappeared from the room, leaving her standing stunned in the middle of the kitchen. She didn't know what to do next, so she finished loading the dishwasher.

Micah returned with a set of sheets. "The sofa pulls out into a bed. You can sleep here."

"But..."

"I'll still pay you. I just don't want you to walk home.

It's too late, and I don't have time to take you. I have to get up early for work."

Katja was about to refuse, but Micah seemed so desperate.

"*Please*," he added. "Stay."

OKAY

Katja didn't know what to make of this turn of events. He said he would pay her for doing *nothing*, and he didn't seem like the type to attack her in her sleep. She had nothing to lose, really. The sofa bed promised to be more comfortable than the lumpy couch she normally slept on. She held out her arms and accepted the bedding.

Once Micah had disappeared behind his bedroom door, Katja padded softly to the bathroom to wash her face. She ran her tongue along her teeth, wishing she had her toothbrush with her. She scrubbed them with a wet finger. That would have to do.

After making the bed, Katja peeled off her tight clothing, laid them on one of the chairs and slipped under the covers wearing only her bra and panties. Her eyes adjusted to the darkness, and she took in the high white ceilings, the dim outdoor light highlighting the windows. Should she text Irma? Let her know she was okay?

She reached for her phone then remembered that she'd thrown it away. It was probably better if she didn't call. Irma and Martina didn't care about her. They'd just be angry if she woke them up or something.

Her eyes cut to the closed door at the end of the hall.

What was Micah's story? Why did he pick her up if he didn't want to take her to bed?

She was grateful, though he may not follow through on his promise to pay her. Even if he did, she still didn't have enough to cover her portion of the rent. She could only hope that her roommates would accept the cash and another IOU. Katja sighed. She'd have to venture out again tomorrow night. Chances are she wouldn't get picked up by two decent guys in a row.

She rolled onto her side and closed her eyes. She mustn't think like that. Things have a way of working out. They always did. She'd laugh about this time in her life one day.

She wiped away a stray tear. Yeah, she'd laugh.

The next morning, she awoke with a start. It took a few moments before she remembered where she was. And why.

She listened carefully for any sounds that would indicate that Micah was still there, but the place was silent. A quick glance into the kitchen confirmed that Micah had eaten breakfast and made coffee—she couldn't believe she'd slept through it.

She grabbed her clothes and rushed her half-naked body across the room and into the bathroom. It was bigger and cleaner than the one she shared with her roommates, and it had a water heating system that wouldn't run out, at least not so fast. It was weird showering in a strange man's stall. She used his soap and shampoo, and dried off with a clean towel. She felt like she'd stayed the night in a hotel and should be the one paying, *not* the one being paid.

She really didn't want to wear her dirty shirt again and briefly considered looting through Micah's closet. He had been so generous already; she couldn't bring herself to do it.

Instead she hand washed her shirt in the sink and laid it over the radiator. As soon as it was dry, she'd leave, but in the meantime it meant hanging out in her bra and short skirt, which wasn't exactly warm. She used the throw blanket from the sofa to wrap herself in. She pushed the bed back to its sofa form and re-arranged the pillows.

The grumbling of her stomach called her to the kitchen. She found a letter on the kitchen table along with a fifty euro note.

Help yourself to breakfast.
  I'll be home at 6:00.
  Micah

Like she'd still be here at six. She stared at the money but didn't touch it. She hadn't earned it, and Micah had already housed and fed her. It just felt wrong to take more from him.

She ate a bun with a piece of ham and a slice of butter cheese and drank a cup of coffee with a good dose of milk and sugar. When she finished, she wiped the counters and washed her dishes, determined to leave the place spotless.

Her shirt was still damp when she checked it, but she found a blow-dryer and turned it on high. She attacked her shirt with hot air for five minutes. It would do.

She put on her jacket and high heels and headed home.

YOU'RE NOT WELCOME

KATJA GASPED when she turned the corner of the hallway that led to the door of her apartment. All her belongings were lying on the floor, including her guitar! She rushed to tug on the handle but the door to the flat was locked. She had been kicked out.

She banged the wall with the fleshy side of her fist, immediately regretting it as the pain shot up her arm. She couldn't fight it this time. Tears streamed down her face. She removed Irma's heels and threw them against the wall at the far end of the hall, letting out an angry cry. She slipped into her own shoes, roughly stuffed her belongings into her duffle bag and zipped it shut. With her heavy bag in one hand and her guitar in the other, she left in a huff.

The frigid wind whistled around the corner and beat against her face. Her hair flew across her eyes and into her mouth. She blew at it unsuccessfully, and had to lower her guitar to clear it. Other people on the street walked briskly, bent over against the cold. She picked up her guitar and walked with her shoulders leaning into the wind.

But where to go?

It was too cold to camp out on a bench or behind a bin. There were shelters for the homeless, but she wasn't ready to consider that just yet, and she didn't exactly know where they were.

Precipitation began to fall in the form of wet snow. She had to get inside somewhere soon before she froze to death.

NOT ONE OF THOSE

SHE'D WALKED the block around Martin Luther Church at least four times. It was her only way to try to keep warm. She glanced up at the dark, imposing cathedral, its spiral poking the winter blue sky, and prayed that God would watch over her.

Or, at least forgive her.

Her fingers were stiff from gripping her scuffed-up guitar case, and her shoulder ached underneath its weight. The bag with all her belongings pulled down on her opposite shoulder. She stopped to rest, rolling her shoulders, rubbing her cold fingers together, swallowing saliva to try to ease her growing thirst, ignoring her hunger. It'd been several hours since she'd eaten breakfast. She hesitated before heading back to *Alaunstrasse*. The row of restaurants and store fronts with open carts of fruit and vegetables taunted her.

Tempted her.

She could just sneak an apple. One apple wouldn't put the vendor out of business but it would fill her shrinking stomach for another day.

But then she'd be a thief.

She may be many things, but she wasn't a thief.

Perhaps she would get lucky and find a half eaten

sandwich or kabob lying out on a sidewalk table, abandoned by the smoker who was forced to eat outside.

It'd happened once.

Worry curled in her chest. She didn't know where she would sleep tonight. Maybe she wouldn't. The parties on *Alaunstrasse* lasted through the night. She could mingle with the crowds, check out some live music.

That was what she was here for, right?

Then she walked by the soup kitchen. The blinds were up on the large, square windows that faced the street, revealing a mid-sized room with wooden tables filled with people eating. A girl, the same one she'd spotted a few days before, sat in the corner playing guitar. She noticed Katja looking in the window, her eyes falling to the guitar case in her hand. The girl smiled and motioned with her head that she should come in.

Katja let out a long breath.

This was a place for poor people.

For homeless people.

She wasn't one of those.

Yet, she was now, wasn't she?

She went in.

THE GIRL WITH THE GUITAR & THE CANE

"Hi, I'm Eva," she said with a smile when Katja walked in. "The soup's free. Make yourself at home."

Katja hesitated in the doorway, feeling even more apprehensive. With the exception of Eva, the people here looked unkempt. The place smelled funny.

Eva didn't sing, just plucked melodies on the strings and strummed. Katja admitted she was pretty good. She could at least stay a while and listen. Warm up.

The girl was thin and looked small behind her big instrument. She had straight brown hair cut bluntly at her shoulder blades and matching blunt bangs that stopped just above her eyebrows. Katja was disappointed when she stopped playing.

The girl set her guitar down awkwardly and then to Katja's surprise, limped noticeably toward a black cane propped in the corner. A shot of anxiety crept up Katja's neck as she watched the girl maneuver off the stage, worried she would fall.

The girl flashed her an embarrassed smile. Then with her free hand, she pointed to the kitchen.

"I'll watch your stuff," she said. "If you want to get something."

Katja glanced around at the others who were finishing

their meals. Spoons scraped along the bottoms of porcelain bowls, and butter knives dropped on the tables after use with the buns. The food looked and smelled okay.

Her hunger beat out her pride.

"Thanks," she said. The soup line was in sight so she kept her eye on her belongings the whole time, but she was grateful that the girl was watching, too.

The place started to empty out by the time Katja began to eat.

"We're closing soon," Eva said, hobbling toward her. Katja looked away from the cane, not wanting to be rude.

"I'll be quick."

"Take your time." Eva pointed to Katja's guitar case. "You play?"

Well, she didn't haul around the heavy instrument for the fun of it. Katja swallowed her soup and nodded. She didn't want to be rude, but she really didn't feel like talking to this girl. She kept her eyes on her food hoping the girl would get the hint, and felt a twinge of regret when the girl left her. Katja cleared her table when she was done and hefted her things back out into the frigid air.

Now what? It didn't take long for the damp cold to seep through her clothing and into her bones. She meandered through a couple shops to warm up. The owners eyed her suspiciously, like she was the type to slip wares into her pocket without paying. She wasn't that type, but she understood the temptation. Would they miss one candy bar? Or a banana?

She was like a bull in a china shop with her bulky guitar case in these small stores. She needed some place bigger, like a mall. She could hang out in the hall and crash on one of the benches. There was a large one in the old town, but it was a cold twenty-minute walk away. Plus, she couldn't live at the mall. She'd have to leave when it closed in a few hours and then where would she go?

She remembered Micah's note. It was humiliating to go back there, but he had extended the invitation, if not directly, definitely by suggestion. At least it would give her time to think. Time to make a new plan.

His place was clean and dry and warm. She was glad she had left the door unlocked. She shoved her things out of sight behind the door. What would Micah do when he discovered she hadn't left? When he found out she was homeless? She hoped he'd let her infringe on his hospitality for one more night.

She groaned. He might cash in on the make out session this time.

She warmed up over the radiator and when she finally felt warm enough, it was almost six o'clock. The least she could do was to prepare *Abendbrot*, a light evening meal of buns and meat and cheese, but decided a warm meal would be a bigger gesture.

She opened all the cupboards, finding them surprisingly bare. A set of dishes for six. Six glasses. Three pots and a frying pan.

There was a little more in the food department, and Katja settled on pasta with Alfredo sauce. She found fresh vegetables in the fridge and prepared a salad while the noodles boiled. Dinner was ready and the table set when Micah walked in.

He jerked to a stop when he saw her, like he'd forgotten that he'd left her sleeping on his sofa bed that morning. His eyes moved to the loaded table.

"Welcome home, sweetie," Katja said lightly. Micah closed the door and set his briefcase on the floor.

"You made dinner," he said, stating the obvious. He removed his jacket and hung it on a hook.

"Yeah, I thought since you made it last night," Katja began, "that it was only fair."

Micah disappeared into the bathroom without another word. Katja folded her arms, preparing herself for the inevitable "time for you to leave" speech.

Instead, Micah took a seat in the same spot as the night before and waited for her to sit across from him.

"Looks good," he said.

"I hope you like it." Katja winced. She felt like she was playing mistress or something.

Micah took a bite and murmured, "Not bad."

It only took one bite of the mushy pasta for her to know he was lying. She'd been telling the truth when she'd said she was a lousy cook. She looked at him apologetically. "It's kind of overcooked."

He took another bite. "It's fine."

"So, how was your day?" she asked politely.

He paused with his fork midair. "Good. Yours?"

Katja couldn't keep her gaze from darting to her things behind the kitchen door. Her guitar case stuck out. Micah's gaze followed hers.

"What's up?" he asked.

"I got kicked out. I couldn't pay my part of the rent… again, and my roommates tossed me." She folded her hands on her lap and stared at the floor. She felt embarrassed and ashamed. What would he say to that?

"Would you like more salad?"

She looked up, shocked, and shook her head. "No, I'm fine."

He set the bowl down. "How old are you, Katja?"

"Twenty. You?"

"Twenty-six." He went to the fridge and removed a bottle of sparkling water. "Want some?"

"You wouldn't happen to have something stronger,

would you?" She flashed a crooked smile. "It's been a hard day. Well, week, actually." She grinned wider. "Okay, month."

He smirked but shook his head. "Sorry, I don't drink. I have orange juice. Would that do?"

She nodded feeling mildly disappointed. "Sure, thanks."

She watched him as he drank his water. His Adam's apple bobbed as he swallowed and she wanted to reach over and loosen his tie. His coal black hair had been professionally cut at one point, but was growing out, and curls formed on his forehead. He moved wayward strands off his brow with one hand. His eyes were a warm, dark brown, yet unreadable.

She couldn't tell what he was thinking.

It drove her crazy.

"What do you want from me?" she blurted.

He sat his water on the table. "What do you mean?"

"I told you I got kicked out. Should I leave? Do you want me to stay? Do you want…?"

He held her gaze, making her squirm. "No, yes… no."

"I don't understand."

"I don't want you on the streets. There's plenty of room here. You can stay until you find something else."

"What's the catch?"

"No catch."

She studied him. There had to be a catch. There was always a catch.

WHAT DRIVES YOU

MICAH STARTED in on the dishes afterward, but Katja stopped him.

"I'll do it." It was the least she could do for the inconvenience she was causing. "You've had a long day already."

"I don't mind," he said, his eyes moving from her to the mess in the sink.

"Neither do I."

He left without another word, and soon Katja heard the sound of the news broadcasting on the TV.

She took her time. It wasn't like she had anything else to do. Micah's flat was spacious, but it didn't actually have a lot of rooms. The living room and kitchen were connected, and there was a short hallway with doors that led to the bathroom and Micah's bedroom. And one other. Perhaps a storage room?

Once the dishes were washed and put away and the counters and table wiped clean, she stood in the middle of the room with a tea-towel in her hand. She didn't want to interrupt Micah, but the living room was the only place left for her to go, unless she holed up in the bathroom. She found a broom in a narrow kitchen closet and attacked the wooden floors. With that done, there really wasn't anything left to do, unless she polished the appliances or washed the windows.

"Looks great." Katja jumped at Micah's voice. "Why don't you come relax now, too?"

As usual, Micah's expression was blank. Katja couldn't tell if he really wanted her to join him, or if he was just being polite.

"Are you sure? I can…" She waved a hand at the spotless room.

"It's clean enough," he said, then returned to his place on the sofa.

Katja wasn't sure if she'd just been invited or instructed to follow him, but she had no reason not to do as he asked.

She sat stiffly on the sofa opposite the chair where Micah sat and steered her gaze to the TV. Her fingers rested on her jeans, and she shifted to get comfortable. Her eyes wouldn't stop veering over to her host. Despite the fact that he rarely smiled, Micah wasn't hard to look at. His brown eyes were accentuated by dark eyebrows. He had sharp cheekbones and a strong jawline now covered by a late-day bristly shadow. Katja's artistic eye captured the details with quick glances, getting caught with her final one. He stared back at her.

She squirmed, feeling stupid that he'd caught her checking him out. His full lips tightened and his shoulders squared, like he refused to be made comfortable, even in his own home. His tie was still tied neatly around his neck. He made her nervous.

"Why don't you take that off?" she blurted.

Micah's eyes widened with surprise, and she couldn't help but laugh. "I meant your tie, not your clothes."

His hand reached for his throat. "Oh. Yeah. I'm so used to wearing it." His fingers slid into the knot loosening it.

"That's better," Katja said. "Now *I* can breathe." She thought it was funny, but Micah didn't crack a smile.

"Are you all right?" she asked.

Micah lowered the volume and tapped his leg nervously with the remote. "Why would you ask?"

Katja nodded to his jumpy hands. "You seem apprehensive. If anyone should be nervous here, it's me, right?" She grinned. "I'm the homeless one."

His hands stilled. "You are. You're taking it rather well."

Oh, no. He thought she was taking advantage of his hospitality already and they hadn't even gotten through the first night. She stiffened. "I've learned to make the best of situations I have no control over."

How did this conversation get turned around to be about her? She tried another tactic. "How long have you lived in Dresden?"

"Four months. You?"

"Two. I arrived the end of January."

"Where from?"

"Berlin."

"That's where your family is?"

Again, it was about her. She nodded and returned the question. "And your family?"

"Hamburg. What's your last name?"

"Stolz. What's yours?"

"Sturm"

Sturm. In English, the word meant storm.

She turned back to the TV, wishing Micah would turn the volume back up. Now he was the one checking her out. She pretended not to notice how his eyes moved from her face, to her chest, along her legs and back again. It both thrilled her and frightened her. She swallowed hard. "Why are you staring at me?"

"What kind of music do you play?"

Fine, don't answer. And if he was going to stare, she'd stare back. "Folk, mostly. A mix of Americana, country, blues."

"Do you write your own songs?"

She nodded. "Yes, but I like to do covers as well."

"And this is the… vocation you've chosen for yourself?" He tilted his head. "When you're not attempting the other one."

She felt herself blush. Her hands curled and her breaths came out in short spurts. She scowled at him. "Are you judging me?"

"No, no." Micah leaned forward placing his elbows on his knees. "I'm sorry I know I can come across as abrasive."

No kidding.

"I'm just trying to understand," he continued. "What drives you to do what you do?"

"I love music. I love to play it. I love how it makes me feel, and how it makes people feel who listen to me. I want to make my living doing it." It sounded straightforward to her.

Again she turned the tables. "What drives you?"

A shadow flickered across his face. He leaned back in his chair, and closed his eyes.

"Micah?"

He stood abruptly and stared at her with a dark and disturbing glare. "What drives me, drives me crazy. Good-night, Katja."

There was definitely a storm brewing in Micah Sturm. Katja wasn't sure she wanted to be around when it was unleashed.

HE'S JUST A FRIEND

KATJA AWOKE mid-morning the next day surprised to see Micah sitting at the table in the kitchen, sipping coffee.

Watching her.

"Good morning," she muttered, feeling self-conscious. Her hand went to her mess of hair, as if patting it would make it look all right. "Why aren't you at work?"

"It's Saturday. I get weekends off."

Oh. Katja often lost track of the days of the week. They all started and ended the same for her.

"There's coffee," Micah offered.

"Thanks. I just need to use the bathroom first." Katja had her sheets gripped in her fist up around her neck. She wore a long T-shirt and panties, but still felt shy about letting Micah see her in her sleepwear. She was aware of the irony.

Micah sensed her hesitation and busied himself at the sink, turning his back to her, giving her the privacy she desired. His consideration for her feelings perplexed her. She didn't understand why he was being so kind and generous without asking for the obvious in return.

Katja grabbed her jeans and a button-down blouse and moved quickly to the bathroom. She was eager to change and make herself presentable, surprising herself by thinking that she wanted to see Micah before he left to do whatever it was he did on Saturdays. Something drew her to him, though she couldn't define what it was.

She felt a strange sense of relief when she found Micah had remained. He sat in his spot at the table with his laptop open, lines drawn on his forehead. He folded it shut when she approached. Whatever it was that he was looking at, he didn't want her to see it.

Her eyes scanned the countertops looking for the promised carafe of coffee, and she squinted when she couldn't find it. "Didn't you mention coffee?"

Micah sprung to his feet. "This is it." He pointed to a rectangular appliance. "It makes one cup at a time." He showed her how to insert the individual coffee pod, placed a clean mug under the spout and pressed a button.

"That's easy enough," Katja said. She took a sip. "Good, too."

"You must eat something, as well," Micah said. He pointed to a small basket of buns on the table. "I visited the bakery this morning."

Katja frowned. She was hungry, but didn't feel right about all this charity. "I have a gig lined up at the Blue Note," she said, taking the seat opposite Micah. "I can pay you something then. And I'll keep looking for gigs. And I'll busk."

"Breathe, Katja," Micah said with a glint of amusement in his eyes. "We'll work something out later." He sipped the remains of his coffee before asking, "What do you mean when you say you'll busk?"

Katja held back a smile. He probably thought it was related to what she'd offered to do for him the night they met. "It's an American term; I'm surprised you haven't heard of it. It's when an artist stands on the street and plays for money. They leave their instrument case open, and if people like what they hear, they'll drop money into it."

Micah nodded. "Oh, I've seen those."

Katja couldn't tell if he approved or not. He was staring at her again. Did he not know that was considered rude? It made her uneasy, and she nibbled on her lip ring in response.

"Did that hurt?" Micah asked.

"What?"

"Piercing your lip like that. I got hit in the face with a football once and split my lip. It hurt like crazy."

Katja shrugged. "Yeah, it hurt."

"Why'd you do it then?"

"I don't know. My friend Henni wanted to do it, so I said I'd do it with her." She boldly held his gaze. "Do you like it?"

"I don't like or dislike it."

Whatever. Katja grabbed a bun and tore a piece off with her teeth.

"So," Micah continued, "what do musicians usually do with their Saturday mornings?"

Thankfully, Katja had plans. "I'm meeting a friend at the Blue Note. We're going to try writing a song together. Maurice Leduc, the manager, he's really cool. He's letting us use the club when it's closed to the public."

"Who's your friend?"

"Sebastian Weiss."

Micah's eyes narrowed. "A guy?"

"Yeah. So?"

Micah leaned back, and his frown grew deeper. Little red flags sprouted in Katja's mind. Was Micah feeling possessive of her already?

"Boyfriend?"

"Seriously, Micah? If he were my boyfriend, would I be staying here with you?"

Micah shrugged. "Maybe he's not a very good boyfriend."

Katja shook her head. How was it their conversations always made her feel like she was under a microscope? "He's just a friend. In fact he has a girlfriend he seems pretty devoted to."

Micah rubbed his face like he was considering the possibility that a guy could be devoted to a girl. Katja took an aggressive bite of her bun.

"I've got errands to run," Micah stated. He washed his cup and plate and placed them on a drying rack. Katja wanted to drill him on the details of his errands in the same way he'd felt free to drill her on her activities, but she kept quiet. She was his guest, and so the onus was on her to be polite.

Katja finished up in the kitchen, cleaning her own dishes, and then tidied up the living room, returning the sofa bed into the sofa position. Micah left without saying another word to her. Had she offended him?

If anyone should be offended, it was her. Katja pushed back at the agitation growing in her gut. She brushed her teeth and ran a brush through her hair one more time, deciding to braid it at the last minute. Finally, it was time to go. She bundled up in her coat and hat, grabbed her guitar and threw herself into the cold wind toward the Blue Note Pub.

When she saw Sebastian there, set up and ready to go, she smiled. Here was someone who understood her, someone who got what she was doing and why. She would push all thoughts of Micah Sturm from her mind and concentrate on music.

Sebastian sat on his amp, guitar in hand, with a far away look on his face. He was remembering something and whatever it was, it wasn't pleasant. Deep lines marked his brow and his blue eyes looked almost black.

Maybe she shouldn't have come? Maybe Micah was right to be concerned about her safety? What did she really know about this guy?

Sebastian spotted her, and his face brightened with a broad, goofy smile. He ran a hand through his messy hair. Along with his wrinkled T-shirt, he looked like he'd just rolled out of bed.

Everything was fine. Sebastian was cool.

"Hey," she said. She pulled off her jacket and carefully removed her hat, patting back loose strands of hair.

"Hey." He strummed his guitar making the peacock tattoo on his arm dance. "Ready to rock?"

Katja snapped her guitar case open, then looked at him. "Oh. I don't do rock."

"It's a figure of speech. Are you ready to get started?"

"Sure." Katja pulled up a chair and settled her guitar on her lap. She ran a few scales to warm up her fingers. "I've only ever written on my own before," she admitted. "I'm not sure what to do."

"Well, do you have any new song ideas? A lyric? Just throw it out there, and we'll see what happens."

Katja paused. Did she have anything? "There was something I heard someone say yesterday."

"Spit it out."

"What drives me, drives me crazy."

"Nice." He plucked out a melody and sang, "What drives me, drives me crazy."

Katja felt the bubble of inspiration stir. "I like it."

They worked on the story about a guy so driven to get

a girl, he almost loses her, and Katja wondered if it didn't contain some of Sebastian's own biography. She enjoyed how they went back and forth, each coming up with lyric ideas for the verses and the chorus, and inspiring each other with new melody lines.

"This is good," Sebastian said. "Just needs a bridge. I really think we might have something here."

Katja felt like laughing. "Me, too."

They both looked up when they heard the door open. A familiar form entered the room and stood at the back.

"Micah?" What was he doing there?

"Is that your boyfriend?" Sebastian asked.

Katja didn't know what he was to her. She nibbled her lip ring and shook her head. "He's just a friend."

Micah approached and reached out to shake Sebastian's hand. "I'm Micah, Katja's roommate."

So that was his title.

"Sebastian, Katja's songwriting partner."

Micah didn't smile at that, and Katja noticed how his gaze settled on Sebastian's tattoo for a moment too long. She didn't think he approved.

"What are you doing here?" she asked.

"I was in the neighborhood…"

Katja found that hard to believe. "We were just finishing up."

"Yeah, our new song is gonna rock," Sebastian said.

"Can I hear it?" Micah asked.

Katja's eyes widened in alarm. "No." She didn't want him to know she took his line. He might not like it. "It's not ready yet."

"She's right, man," Sebastian said. "It needs more work before it's ready to showcase." He put his gear away. "I gotta run, Katja."

Sebastian had the keys to the club, so Katja had to

leave as well. She packed up her guitar and grabbed her things.

She wasn't sure how she felt about Micah showing up uninvited, but part of her liked that he was concerned about her. Even if he was just a friend.

EMPTY WALLS

They fell into a domestic routine. She slept on the sofa bed, and he in his room behind a closed door. He left for work before she woke up. At first he bought groceries, and she'd make dinner, but after a run of poorly cooked meals culminating in a recent meal of undercooked rice and burned steak, Micah suggested they reverse roles. She suggested they go back to the traditional lighter evening meal since it was pretty much impossible for her to screw up, but Micah said he grew up eating the American way, with a hot meal at the end of the day. If she would do the shopping for the meal, he'd cook it.

It was nice. And odd.

And she found she thought about Micah Sturm way more throughout her lonely days than she should. She'd convinced herself that the idea of anything developing between them was ridiculous and that any attraction she felt ran only one way. But then he'd unabashedly stare at her, tossing her theory. She knew how men looked at her when they desired her. She'd caught Micah with that same look.

But he'd kept his distance, both physically and emotionally. If that was what he wanted, Katja would comply.

Katja noticed things about Micah's flat she hadn't in the first couple days. Like, even though the furniture was nice and new, there wasn't much of it. There weren't any decorations or souvenirs. No personal photographs of family or friends. Not one picture hung on the walls.

It was like he was ready to pack and move at a moment's notice.

The high ceilings and large windows made the space seem bigger than it was. Besides the kitchen, living room and bathroom, there was Micah's bedroom.

And the room with a locked door.

Katja tried the knob every day simply because she was curious. What did Micah have in there? Why did he feel like he had to keep it locked?

Micah was a very private man. She didn't dare ask him. Besides, it was none of her business.

She spent the mornings working on music and the afternoon's trying to line up gigs. She got a few, and the one at the Blue Note was coming up next week.

Sometimes she would busk and she always tried to give her earnings to Micah. He refused to take them, so she used the money to buy groceries and put the remainder in the fruit bowl on the table for the rent. Micah frowned when he saw it, but said nothing. He never took the money, either.

Every other evening or so, Micah's cell phone would ring, and he'd disappear into his bedroom. At first Katja thought he had a long-distance girlfriend somewhere. She imagined he wouldn't be telling her about his female room-mate sleeping on the sofa bed. The thought of another girl out there had a weird effect on Katja's nerves. She felt strangely jealous, though she knew she had no right to be.

Then one night, she heard Micah slip and refer to the mystery caller as "Mama." At first Katja smiled to herself.

Of course, Micah Sturm was a mama's boy. But again, she wondered if he'd told his mother about her, or if she was just another one of his secrets.

She decided she wasn't waiting on his company again. He had a right to hole up in his room and talk on the phone, and she had the right to leave. She put on a light coat and tugged a twenty euro note out of the fruit bowl and slipped it into her pocket. It was open mic night at the Blue Note. She eyed her guitar as she headed for the door. No, tonight she wouldn't play. She'd just listen. And drink. Micah didn't want alcohol in the house, which was fine, but sometimes a girl just needed a shot.

She walked briskly toward the center of *Neustadt*, breathing heavily through her nose. She pushed at the strong feelings of discontent that brewed in her stomach. Not only because she hadn't made any real progress on her "career" since she started staying with Micah, but also because of *Micah*.

He was the complete opposite of her in every way. Where she was outgoing, he was a homebody. Where she was a creative, right-brained thinker, he was a left-brained numbers guy. Where she was poor, he was rich.

She had a naturally happy disposition, and he was undeniably melancholy.

So why was she *attracted* to him?

That was the truth. She *liked* Micah Sturm, and it irked her that he apparently had no such struggles concerning her. And if he did, he hid them well. And why would he find it necessary to bury them? Unless he felt she was beneath him. She *had* offered him love for money. Probably not a characteristic he'd be looking for in a girlfriend. Her emotions were in a tight ball of hurt and frustration. Just how much rejection could a person take?

Herr Leduc welcomed her with a kiss on both cheeks.

He folded his arms over his round body, his eyes landing on her empty hands. "*Ma Cherie*, you're not playing for us tonight?"

Katja smiled and shrugged. "I need to give other people a turn, Herr Leduc. I'm here to listen."

"Please, call me Maurice."

She went inside and searched for a friendly face. She frowned when her eyes settled on Irma and Martina on the far side of the room. She hadn't seen them since the night before they'd locked her out. Irma nudged Martina with an elbow and they snickered.

Sebastian and Yvonne were sitting at a table at the back. She moved toward them and felt immensely relieved and thankful when Sebastian smiled warmly at her. "Katja! Join us!"

She sat across from them beside a tall, skinny guy with dark, messy hair. Sebastian had introduced her to him before, but she didn't remember his name.

Sebastian came to her rescue. Again. "Karl-Heinz, you remember Katja?"

"Sure. Hello."

"Karl-Heinz is the drummer in our band. We're called the Hollow Fellows."

Katja laughed. "Great name. I can't wait to hear you play."

"At small gigs like this, KH and I play as a duo. Next week our band plays at Alexandra's. You should come."

"I'll try."

To Karl-Heinz he said, "Katja and I are writing this wicked song."

Karl-Heinz nodded. "Cool." Yvonne rolled her eyes.

The server came to their table and Katja ordered a glass of wine, downing half of it the moment it arrived. It'd been a long time since she had a drink and she loved how it burned slightly as it went down and left a warm glow to her cheeks.

Maurice introduced the first player, a guy with a beard and a wool cap, and the room quieted. That was the nice thing about playing to other musicians. They all understood how important it was to respect the artist by listening.

He was good, and everyone cheered when he finished his two song set. The next artist went on stage. Katja finished her drink and ordered another. She felt relaxed and happy. She was in her element, in a room full of people who were like her.

She smiled at Sebastian and Karl-Heinz. Yvonne didn't smile in return, but at least she'd stopped scowling. They were her *friends*.

She had *friends*.

She had another drink and then leaned across the table toward Sebastian. "When do you play?" She heard the slur in her voice, but it just made her giggle.

"I think we're next."

Sure enough, Maurice called them to the stage. Katja cheered loudly. She loved her *friends*!

She already knew from their songwriting session that Sebastian had a great rock voice, but it was even better in this performance. Karl-Heinz played a cool back beat to the song on a beat box. The song was new to her. It was *fantastic*.

Katja leaned toward Yvonne. "I've never heard this before. Did he write it?"

Yvonne raised an eyebrow Katja wasn't sure why. Was she talking too loud? Yvonne nodded looking bored. She'd probably heard this song a zillion times.

When Sebastian and Karl-Heinz got off the stage,

Katja threw herself at them, giving them each a big hug. "That was so great! You guys are so great!"

Sebastian laughed. "Katja! You're a happy drunk."

She wobbled on her feet. "I'm not drunk."

He laughed again and helped her to her chair. "If you say so."

She wasn't drunk. Was she? She ran her hands through her hair and then rested her face in her palms, elbows on the table. Her face felt thick, and she was light-headed and woozy. Maybe she was drunk.

Oh, no. What would Micah think?

Who *cared* what Micah thought? He didn't own her. He didn't *love* her. She could get drunk if she wanted to.

"I'm going home," she announced. She struggled into her jacket and waved goodbye, stopping at the bar to buy a bottle for the road. She wasn't driving. It was okay.

Somehow she managed to stay on the sidewalks. Even this late at night, there were loads of people out and about. A lot of them walking with open drinks in their hands.

Hey, she was thirsty, and she had a bottle of wine in her hand. Thank God for twist caps! She opened the bottle and took a long swig. Somehow she found her way back to Micah's flat. She was like a freaking homing pigeon! She didn't even have to think and, voila, here she was.

She had Sebastian's song in her head, and she sang it as she climbed the steps. The stairwell had great acoustics, and she belted it out.

Micah was waiting for her at the top of the stairs. The door to his apartment was open. He had his arms folded over his chest and a frown on his pretty face.

"What's wrong?" Katja simpered.

"It's late. I don't think the neighbors appreciate being serenaded in the middle of the night." Micah guided her inside and closed the door. "Why didn't you tell me you were going out? I was worried."

"Oh, you were?" Katja leaned against him heavily. She stroked his face. "I'm so sorry, I worried you. Here…" she held up her open bottle. "Have a drink."

Micah took the bottle and set in on the table.

"Wait," she said, reaching. "I want more."

"I think you've had enough."

Katja furrowed her brow and stuck out her bottom lip. "You're mad, aren't you? I've disappointed you."

"I think you should go to sleep now." Micah walked her over to the sofa bed. He opened it and helped her to lie down.

She propped herself up on an elbow. "What are we Micah? What *are* we?"

"We're friends."

She pouted. "Just friends? I *like* you, Micah. And I know you like me." She patted the spot beside her. "Come. It'll be fun."

Micah hesitated, then to her absolute delight, he slid in beside her. Not close enough to touch, but close enough that she smelled mint toothpaste on his breath, saw his chest rise and fall, noticed the gold flecks around his irises. She laid a hand over his heart and felt his heartbeat speed up. He shuddered as her finger drew the shape of a crescent moon along his ribcage.

His mouth brushed against her ear, and she shivered. "I'm sorry Katja," he whispered. "This isn't right."

What?

He shifted back, avoiding her eyes, and swallowed. "I have to go."

"No, wait." Katja felt the panic that preceded imminent rejection. "Why?"

"Because you're drunk, and… just because."

Micah sprung to his feet and walked toward his bedroom. Katja threw a cushion, hitting him on the back of the head. "You're such a party pooper."

He stopped but didn't turn around. "Good night, Katja."

EVERYTHING & NOTHING

KATJA AWOKE the next morning to the aroma of strong coffee. The bright light pouring in from the windows hurt her eyes, and she whipped an arm over her face to shield them.

What happened last night?

Then she remembered everything—talking loudly and loosely at the Blue Note, throwing herself at Sebastian in front of his girlfriend. She groaned. Yvonne was sure to hate her now.

Oh, no. She came on to Micah. She'd felt so pretty and captivating but now she knew she'd looked wrecked like a cheap drunk, slurring her words and stumbling over her feet. Ugh. She felt so stupid and embarrassed.

She dared to look around. The time on the clock above the stove told her that Micah had left for work long ago. She pulled herself to her feet and stumbled to the bathroom. Her stomach swirled and her head pounded.

She moaned when she saw her image in the mirror. Mascara smudged down her cheeks and around her bloodshot, hazel eyes. Her hair was a rat's nest. She swallowed two Tylenol and took a long shower.

Once dressed, she made herself a cup of coffee. It was

extra bitter and strong, but exactly what she needed to get her going.

How was she going to face Micah after her ridiculous behavior? Any chance of winning his affections and becoming more than friends was long gone now. The most she could do was make herself presentable and useful to have around.

To that end, she brushed and blow-dried her hair and applied a small amount of make-up. She cleaned the bathroom and straightened the living room. The kitchen was already spotless. Her half-empty bottle of wine sat beside the microwave. She almost dumped it, but couldn't face pouring good money down the drain. She put it in one of the cupboards out of sight. Her stomach was ready for a little food, so she ate a piece of toast, washing her plate and knife immediately afterward.

Now what to do? Laundry? She could wash his clothes, but that would mean going into his bedroom, and she didn't feel comfortable doing that. She dusted the TV and the end tables, pausing at the mystery door to see if it was still locked.

Yup.

She sat on the sofa and stared at the bare walls.

And she got an idea.

Taking her sketch pad and drawing pencils, she headed out into the spring sunshine, wearing a light jacket with her torn jeans. She planted her sunglasses firmly on her face. It was a short walk to the park, where she claimed one of the few empty benches. She wasn't the only artist to be found along the banks of the River Elbe capturing the landmarks on paper. After sketching out the skyline to her satisfaction, she walked across the bridge, pausing near the arched gateway to the old town to sketch a street musician playing the violin. Then she continued on, entering the city square that surrounded the *Frauenkirche*. A dog lying in the sun at its owner's feet at an outdoor café caught her interest. She sat at a table across from them and ordered an espresso, and busily sketched the dog while sipping at it.

She had three sketches she liked when she headed for a euro store to buy frames and finishing nails. She knew Micah had a small tool kit in the bathroom beside the washing machine. It had to have a hammer in it.

When she got back to the flat she chose a bare wall in the living room and hung her three framed sketches in a cluster. She smiled with satisfaction. They looked good there.

It was almost six and Katja wanted to make dinner for Micah for a change. She cubed the chicken breasts she'd found, added a jar of curry sauce and simmered it on the back of the stove. She kept her attention on the task at hand. She didn't want to burn or overcook anything this time. She made a pot of rice, timing it precisely, and prepared a salad. She grabbed a couple bills from the fruit bowl and raced to the bakery café around the corner. She bought a fresh loaf of bread and two slices of apple cake for dessert.

When she returned, she smelled smoke. Oh no! She should've turned the chicken down. She quickly moved the pan off the element and opened the windows. What was she thinking? Did she want to burn the place down?

This was not exactly the scene she wanted Micah to come home to. What now?

She dialed the number for the Thai restaurant down the street. If she hurried she could be back before Micah got home.

Somehow she managed to have the table set including a new bottle of sparkling water, when Micah arrived.

"Hey," he said when their eyes met. His gaze moved from her to the dinner waiting on the table.

"Hey," she said. She felt nervous and embarrassed. "It's just takeout."

Micah set his briefcase down and removed his suit jacket. "I'll wash up first."

"Okay." Katja sat in what had become her place at the table. Micah returned wearing jeans and his dress shirt untucked. His top button was undone. No tie.

Katja gulped. He was so attractive.

She managed to find a few words. "How was your day?" Okay, they were lame words.

"Good. And yours?"

Really, they already sounded like a boring old married couple.

"Look, Micah," Katja started. "About last night."

Micah's eyes glistened with amusement. "It's fine, Katja. You went out. You had fun."

"Still, I should've told you. I should've *invited* you. I don't usually drink that much. I don't know what got into me."

He grinned. "It's okay. You were cute."

Katja's jaw dropped. Did he really just say that?

Micah turned his attention to the meal in front of him and dug in. She wished that he'd keep talking, or at least ask her questions, but he seemed okay with the silence.

"I have something to show you," Katja said after they were finished eating. He followed her into the living room, and she showed him the wall. Micah's expression remained staid as he stared at her sketches. She worried that he didn't like them, or worse that he was angry she'd taken it upon herself to hang art without asking.

"I'm sorry. I shouldn't have assumed," she mumbled.

"No, no. They're great." He turned to her, taking in

her face. "You're really talented. Not just with music, it seems."

Katja felt her lips tug up. A compliment from Micah meant the world. "Thanks."

Just when she thought their relationship might take a turn, Micah's cell rang. His mother again. He disappeared into his room, and twenty minutes later he returned, turned on the TV and watched the news.

It was just like any other night. Nothing had changed.

The next morning, Katja sat at the kitchen table, her notebook opened up to a new page, her pen lying beside it. She picked out notes on her guitar and hummed, then she gripped her pen and started scribbling.

> *Friend, won't you calm my mind*
> *I feel like it will implode*
> *The difference between you and I*
> *Is like the sun and the moon*

She nibbled on her pen, considering Micah and how different they were from each other. If she were smart, she would leave this place. If he were smart, he'd make her.

> *And you know, you should know*
> *That to stop just means you should go*
> *(I should go)*
> *We live in different worlds*

She quit when she noticed the time. She had a half-hour slot booked to busk in the square in the old town. It was her first time to get this location, and it was prime for busking with a lot of pedestrians, especially this time of year. She put away her notepad and packed up her guitar. It was a fifteen-minute walk, and her arms would burn by the time she got there. She needed to arrive with enough time to let them recover.

It was warm enough now that she no longer needed gloves, which made playing much easier. The strings didn't go out of tune so quickly. She opened her case, dropping a few coins in, strapped the guitar on, checked the tuning and began to play. Most of the people kept walking by on their way to shop, or to work, or to sight-see, but some stopped to listen, and a few threw money into the case.

Her eyes scanned the crowd, and she felt happy to play for so many people, even if they weren't exactly listening.

Then her gaze landed on a familiar face, and her heart stuttered.

Micah.

He stood there in his blue suit jacket, a white cotton scarf around his neck, and dress pants that hung perfectly over leather shoes. The breeze blew curls off his face.

How long had he been watching her?

And why did she care? Why did his presence make her pulse race? It wasn't like he hadn't heard her play before, but it was the first time he'd seen her in action on the street. This was her turf, and it was far from the wealthy, sterile world of banking.

What was he doing here?

Then she remembered he worked at a bank in the center of the old town.

She closed her eyes and concentrated on her song. When she opened them, he was still there watching. She looked for a sign that he enjoyed what he heard and what he saw, but his brow inched down and his eyes narrowed.

He didn't understand her. He thought she was a fool.

Maybe she was.

He left before she finished, so she didn't get a chance to talk to him. She bought groceries with the money she'd earned, and he made dinner when he got home, just like usual. She didn't say anything about seeing him at the square. She didn't think he would say anything either. Micah was consistently the strong, silent type, but that night he proved her wrong.

"Why?" he asked simply.

"Why what?"

"Why are you doing this? I mean, I get that you like to play guitar and write songs, and you're good, but making a living as a musician is obviously very, very hard."

Obviously.

"So, you think I should be a secretary or a nurse or something and just do music for fun?"

Micah shrugged. "Why not? At least then you'd be able to support yourself."

It was like a cement truck backed into the room and started dumping when he said that. Katja caught her breath. "I'll leave in the morning."

"No, I didn't…"

Katja stood and started clearing the table. "It's fine. I've overstayed my welcome. I get it."

She felt a tug on her arm. Micah towered over her, his head tilting, a look of remorse on his face. "I didn't mean to offend you, Katja. I'm just trying to understand." The melancholy he'd been masterfully hiding returned to his eyes. "Why did you leave home?"

She found his nearness intoxicating. She backed up, shaking it off. This quiet, sad man was not for her.

He ducked to force her to look into his eyes. "Help me to understand."

She gave him a sharp look. "My stepfather and I don't get along. Let's just say he wants more from our relationship than I'm willing to give." Katja blinked hard. She couldn't believe she just blurted that out. That was private and none of his business.

Anger flashed behind Micah's dark eyes. "I see."

She turned. "It doesn't matter."

"Of course it does. Have you reported him?"

She hadn't. It would only cause more trouble. Just another thing he couldn't understand about her. "Can we drop it? I didn't mean to bring it up."

"Okay."

She wanted to say something to remove the dark, heavy blanket that had fallen over them. "Come to my gig at the Blue Note." Maybe that would help him to understand.

Micah's gazed softened, but he didn't quite smile. "I'll be there."

THE BLUE NOTE

KATJA TOLD Micah she had to leave early to set up. It was true, but she also didn't want him to feel like this was a date.

Maurice let her in, giving her a friendly, boisterous pep talk, and she set up her stuff on the stage. A guy named Holgar set up the house sound system and she tested the mic. The guitar sounds bounced off the walls, but that would fix itself when the room filled.

Hopefully, it would fill.

What if no one showed? No one but Micah? That would be so embarrassing and further prove his point that she should do something more responsible with her life.

She breathed deeply with relief when people started showing up and the seats filled. She recognized the regulars, including Sebastian and his gang, and waved as they walked in. She froze to the spot when Micah entered. He was dressed casually in jeans and a button-down shirt. He looked freshly showered. He drew a hand through his hair when he spotted Katja, messing it in a way that made her heart skip a beat.

She finally came to her senses and pulled her gaze away. In her peripheral vision, she saw him slip into a seat at the back. He ordered a cola, and then stared at her as she continued to set up.

She swallowed and fought back her nerves. She was a professional. She could do this.

After testing her mic and strapping on her guitar, she nodded to Maurice, letting him know she was ready.

"Ladies and gentlemen," Maurice bellowed out with his warm, friendly voice. "I'm pleased to introduce to you an incredible new talent. I'm sure she will go places! Help me in welcoming Katja Stoltz!"

She waited for the applause to end, then said, "Thank you for having me. I'm opening this night with a new song. It's dedicated to my friend, Micah."

Katja caught his eye and swore she even saw his lips tug up into a slight smile.

> *Friend, won't you calm my mind*
> *I feel like it will implode*
> *The difference between you and I*
> *Is like the sun and the moon*
> *And you know, you should know*
> *That to stop just means you should go*
> *I should go*
> *We live in different worlds*

> *It is obvious*
> *that one of them makes*
> *the other one feel small and cold*
> *Let me dream further,*
> *I need more*
> *And you know*
> *that I'm living on the moon*

She sang through her list of songs and though she worked to engage the crowd, the only person she really cared about sat alone in the back corner of the room.

Maurice congratulated her on her set, and the crowd swarmed her when she stepped off the stage to buy her CDs and to get autographs. She kept looking at Micah from the corner of her eye, and he raised his empty glass to her.

Sebastian approached and gave her a hug. "That was amazing. I love that *Sun and Moon* tune. It rocked!" She laughed at his enthusiasm, and turned back to see Micah's expression, but his table was empty. He'd left.

A wave of disappointment washed over her. Of course he wouldn't stay to the dire end. This wasn't his scene. Plus, if he walked her home, it might look like they were together. She understood if he didn't want to accidentally run into someone he knew with her alone at his side.

She packed up her guitar and remaining CDs, pocketed her earnings and accepted the complimentary beer Maurice offered her.

She took her time walking home, needing to unwind from the adrenaline rush that a concert brought on. It was a good night. She was good, her songs were good, and the crowd loved her. Micah saw that, at least.

He was sitting on the steps of his apartment building when she got there. She smiled widely, surprised but happy to see him there. She set the case down and sat beside him.

"The sun and moon aren't mutually exclusive," he said. "They need each other."

His dark eyes locked on hers.

"I know," she whispered.

He leaned toward her, reaching up to stroke her cheek.

His touch was like a bolt of lightning. Searing heat tingled through her whole body. His lips hovered above hers, teasing. He was going to kiss her and she wanted him to. She'd wanted him to kiss her for a long time now.

Her heart stammered, and she held her breath. She was ready to close her eyes when he suddenly pulled back.

"Micah?"

He rubbed his face with his hands, standing briskly. His expression tensed with a flash of anguish in his eyes, like he was torn. His eyes flickered to the ground, then down the road and up at the sky. Everywhere but at her.

"We should go in," he said stiffly, hopping the steps to the door and opening it. Katja grabbed her guitar, wide-eyed with confusion, and followed after him.

What just happened?

THE DOOR

Micah disappeared into his room and never came out again. Katja's annoyance turned to anger. Just who did he think he was? If he didn't want to kiss her, she didn't want to kiss him, either. They were roommates, nothing more.

She tossed and turned on the sofa bed. Normally, she had no trouble falling asleep but tonight was different.

It was a full moon. The moonbeams reached in through the window and stroked her face.

He was the moon.

Micah's gravitational pull gripped and stretched her. He was nothing like anyone she'd ever met before. He was darkness and light, sadness and hope. A complete enigma.

His bedroom door creaked open, and she squeezed her eyes shut, pretending to sleep. She expected him to pad into the bathroom, but he turned left instead of right. She heard a key turn a lock.

She opened her eyes to slivers, catching his form as he disappeared into the locked room, closing the door softly behind him.

Part of her wanted to jump up and follow him. *What was in there?*

She sat up, her gaze never leaving the crack of light

coming from under the closed door. Should she go? She would knock first. Would he let her in? Would he be angry?

The questions flooded her brain. All the while her body managed to balance on the squishy surface of her bed. She tugged the long T-shirt over her butt and stepped onto the floor.

She could find her way to the bathroom in the dark with her eyes closed, but the locked room was on the opposite side. Katja fumbled her way around the furniture, catching her toe on a chair leg.

She cried out in pain.

Immediately, the light under the door went out and Micah appeared in the hallway. He quickly closed and locked the door, and when he turned to her, the moonlight landed on his panic-stricken face.

Katja held her foot, rubbing her toe vigorously, before letting it go. "What's in there, Micah?"

"It's nothing." His eyes moved to her bare legs, and then back to her face. "I'm sorry I woke you." He turned, and disappeared into his room, leaving Katja feeling more curious and more disturbed than ever.

COFFEE SHOP ON THE CORNER

Working alone in Micah's apartment day after day became too dreary for Katja. Tired of staring at white walls and being taunted by the locked door, she'd begun to frequent the coffee shop on the corner. It was brightly painted with a warm and welcoming atmosphere, and the smell of the in-house bakery was heavenly. Here she could enjoy a cup of coffee that tasted as good as the ones she made with the fancy machine at Micah's, and she could people watch, too.

Katja ordered milk coffee and a scone with butter and jam from a slender, middle-aged woman who she'd come to know as Frau Renata Beck. Frau Beck wore the standard black skirt, white shirt uniform with the café-specific apron, tied her greying hair in a low ponytail and wore sensible shoes. She also liked to laugh, as did Katja, and they often joked around about tabloid news, and cooed together at cute babies who arrived in strollers with their mothers. Before too long, they were on a first name basis as friends.

People were fascinating, and in Dresden there were all kinds. Katja sipped her coffee while gazing at the interesting characters outside the window. There was the attractive, hippy owner of the import gift shop across the street sitting on a collapsible wooden stool, smoking a cigarette.

He snubbed it out and followed two young women dressed in jeans and trendy jackets, tourists likely, back into the shop. In the park next door, a group of punks stood around an old boom box. They had spiky Mohawks on their heads and dog collars around their necks and actual, sizable dogs dozing at their feet. A white-haired woman with a cane stopped to examine the produce on a sidewalk display outside an organic produce store. It was run by a very small Asian woman who came outside to assist her.

The energy was inspiring. Katja always brought her notebook to scribble down song ideas and lyrics, and her sketchbook to draw in. She did a lot of faces. Her unsuspecting subjects stood in line at the coffee shop waiting to order, or quietly drank their beverages and ate their desserts at nearby tables, believing they were alone and unnoticed.

Renata wiped the empty table next to the one Katja sat at. "*Schatz*," she said with a look of concern. "Are you all right? You look unsettled." She was more motherly toward Katja than her own mother ever was, and it both eased her pain and added to it.

The events of the night before weighed heavily on Katja, and she had difficulty hiding her emotions from this woman. Still, she couldn't confide in her. What would she say? She lived with a guy she barely knew who had a mystery room he kept locked? If she were Renata, she'd be telling herself to get packed and moved, pronto.

Not only that. Today was her birthday and she had no one to share it with. She supposed it would be okay to let her know that.

"It's my birthday, Renata."

"Oh, *Engel*." Angel. Renata dropped her cloth and swooped down to hug her young friend. "All the best!"

She pulled back and stared Katja in the eyes. "Birthdays can be harder than they are happy sometimes, isn't it true? But let me get you a piece of apple cake, my gift. That will cheer you up, yes?"

Katja forced a wide smile. "That's sweet of you."

"Something sweet for someone sweet, *Süße*."

Unlike most Germans, Renata loved to use nicknames. Treasure, angel, and now sweetness. Katja couldn't stop the smile that spread across her face.

Renata squeezed her shoulders. "Your face just lights up when you smile," she said. "You must do it more often."

Katja knew her broad smile was one of her distinguishing features. You had to know these things about yourself as an artist. It was a tool she'd used to disarm many a guy, teacher, employer… even her step-father. A move that had backfired.

She pushed thoughts of him away, but she couldn't help thinking about her mother and sister. Had they even remembered that today was her birthday?

Didn't matter. Today she would be happy. She would fulfill her role as the sun.

Katja picked up her sketching pencil and began stroking the blank page in front of her. She started with long curving lines that turned into an orb. She divided it in half with a concave line. On the wide side, she added the flares of the sun. On the concave side, the shadows of the moon. The images became faces, facsimiles of her adventure-seeking eyes and Micah's compassionate gaze. Her smile and his frown.

She pulled back and studied it. Her lips tugged up, and she let her smile take over her face. She liked it.

Katja took time to savor the apple cake, enjoying each bite until she finished. Then she cleared her mess away, gathered her things and waved good-bye to Renata. She wanted to busk at the bridge during the afternoon, so she had to go back to Micah's apartment to fetch her guitar. The morning had started out grey and gloomy, but now the sun was peeking out. She could trade her jacket for a sweater and leave her scarf at home.

She brushed her teeth and her hair and applied a little makeup. Before she left, she took another look at her sketch. She added a title, *Sun & Moon*, dated it and signed it. Then, after deliberating for a few minutes, she taped it to the surface of the locked door.

BIRTHDAY GIRL

THE COMBINATION of a beautiful afternoon and her determination to smile brightly paid off. Her busking donations were better than they'd ever been since she arrived in Dresden, and she sold two CDs.

That meant she could afford a cake. She stopped at the bakery on the way home and chose a small one—there was only the two of them to eat it—that was dark and chocolatey and creamy. She wrestled with balancing the precious package while carrying her guitar, opening doors and maneuvering up the steps to the flat, until she had it safely landed on Micah's kitchen table.

She decided to make dinner, but this time she lit a candle and turned on the satellite music station to a soft jazz channel.

Micah couldn't contain his surprise when he got home. His eyes flickered and his lips twitched. "What's this?"

Katja immediately suspected that Micah felt he was getting railroaded into a type of date, and she hurried to calm his fears. "It's nothing. Just, it's my birthday. I thought we could celebrate, but if it's too much..." She blew out the candle feeling stupid. Why did she even tell him it was her birthday? Weren't things already awkward enough after last night?

"Katja, why didn't you tell me sooner?" Micah picked up the lighter and relit the candle. "Happy Birthday!" he said in English. Then he smiled. Actually, full-out smiled! Katja thought it was the best birthday gift he could've given her. But then he surprised her again. "Wait here," he said, before disappearing into his bedroom.

Like she had anywhere to go.

He emerged with his tie off, shirt untucked and a small package in his hand.

Katja was confused. How could he already have a gift when he didn't even know it was her birthday?

"I bought this for you a while ago," Micah explained. He jutted his hand out to give it to her. "After that night when you left without telling me and came home late."

Katja blushed. "I remember. I'd had too much to drink."

"Yeah, well, I hated that I couldn't call or text you."

"So you bought me a phone?" Katja was touched. It wasn't fancy or expensive, just a pre-paid kind, but still, it meant Micah cared about her. Her throat grew scratchy and she found it hard to swallow.

"I didn't know if you'd appreciate it," Micah added, "and there never seemed to be a good time to ask you. Before now."

"Thank you," she said. "I do appreciate it." She looked at him, not knowing what the protocol between them was. Should she hug him? Kiss his cheeks? Do nothing?

Micah answered her by sitting down. "It's my pleasure. Now you have no excuse to let me worry about you."

A bubbly joy spouted up in Katja's belly. Someone worried about her. *Micah* worried about her. It felt good.

They dug into the simple meal of pork cutlets with potatoes. Katja wrinkled her top lip. The meat was on the dry side. "I'm sorry. I don't know why I keep trying."

Micah grunted happily. "You can't be good at everything."

Katja supposed he was right. Micah poured two glasses of sparkling water and she took a sip of hers. "We'll need the whole bottle to get this dinner down," she joked.

He motioned to her new phone. "You could call your mother. I'm sure she'd like to hear from you on your birthday."

Katja rested her fork on her plate in slow motion. "I doubt she even remembers."

Micah considered her. "You're her daughter," he said softly. "I'm sure she remembers. Call her."

Katja stared at her hands, her happiness draining from her.

Micah startled her by shifting over to the empty chair closest to her. He stared into her eyes. "What happened?"

Katja supposed he found it odd that she never communicated with her mother, especially in light of the fact that he talked to his all the time.

"My father left my mother and me when I was five," she began. "For a couple of years it was just the two of us, and it was okay. At least I thought it was okay. I didn't know my mother had started taking pills to cope with her growing depression. Then one day, seemingly out of the blue, she married Horst."

Katja didn't know why she was telling Micah this. He was pretty tight-lipped about his own secrets, but now that she'd started, she couldn't seem to stop.

"Horst was nice enough at first," she added. "Always bringing me candies and small toys. Then I noticed my mother was getting large in the stomach, and soon afterward my sister Sibylle was born.

"Mama never lost her baby weight, and I grew into my curves. Horst's affections moved from my mother to me.

He was always touching me and flirting with me. Mama was too drugged up by this time to notice, and when I tried to talk to her about it, she called me an ungrateful liar.

"She was just scared. I know that now. She had no way of supporting us without Horst. She lost her job, and eventually she stopped coming out of her room. She barely got out of bed. I was used to the house being empty after school. Sibylle learned to go to our neighbor's flat until Horst came home.

"One day Horst came home from work early. He'd gotten laid off from his job and had been drinking. When he laid his glassy-eyed glare on me, his lips pulling up into a smarmy smile, I knew I was in trouble. I ran to my room, but I wasn't fast enough. I tried to block the door with the dresser but he pushed it open and then shoved me onto my bed."

Katja dared to look at Micah and then closed her eyes. She couldn't bear to see his pity. He gripped her hand and squeezed.

The emotions of that moment flooded back like the attack had happened yesterday: Horst's heavy body pinning her down, his putrid breath choking her, the stench of his hand clasped over her mouth, and the fear that exploded in her mind, incapacitating her. The way he thrust his meaty hand under her shirt, scratching her flesh with jagged nails. How she trembled with disgust when it found its way under her bra and squeezed her breast. The shameful and filthy way she felt being touched by him. His dry, ropy lips on her neck.

She swallowed hard at the memories. A quiet sob escaped her lips. "I squirmed and tried to fight back, but he weighed twice as much as me. My mother was passed out from pills in the next room. She was *there*, but couldn't help me.

73

"And then a miracle happened. My friend Henni stopped by. I'd taken her math textbook by accident. She knew I was usually home alone after school, so she just walked in, looking for me. She appeared at my doorway before Horst could move. He was so drunk, he just started laughing at the shock on her face. Like being caught trying to rape your step-daughter was hilarious."

Katja's hazel eyes were wet with tears. "That's why I can't go back. That's why I can't call."

Micah nodded with understanding. "What about your sister? Is she safe?"

"I hope so. She's actually his blood daughter. I'm not related to him, except through marriage. I don't think he'd touch her. Besides, she's only eleven." Horst was a pervert, but he wasn't a pedophile. She'd found his stack of dirty magazines. He liked his women post pubescent.

She fiddled with the phone. "I'll call her one day. Soon. Just not today."

Micah reached an arm around her and pulled her into a warm embrace. Katja's chin pressed into his shoulder and she breathed deeply of his scent—the musky soap she secretly sniffed in the shower. In his arms she felt safe and protected. She felt valued.

"I'm glad you're here," Micah whispered in her ear. He stroked her hair, then pulled back and reached into his pocket.

Katja sighed. Of course, his mother would ruin a moment like this. But instead of answering, he tapped at the number pad. Suddenly another shrill sound came from her lap, scaring her. Then she laughed. Her new phone was ringing. No one even knew about this phone except Micah. She winked at him and answered, "Katja Stoltz."

"Hi, Katja," Micah said. "Did I hear something about cake?"

CHOCOLATE CAKE & NEW YORK CITY

Katja cut the cake, and Micah poured her a glass of wine from what was left-over from her night of shame. She raised an eyebrow when he handed it to her.

"No reason why you shouldn't have a glass of wine on your own birthday," he said.

She eyed the green bottle, noting that there was enough left for a second glass. "And you won't join me?"

He shrugged. "Nah. It's not my thing."

She took the glass from him, not taking her gaze off his while she sipped the wine. "Thank you."

The chemistry between them sizzled. She wanted to grab him and plant a wet one right on his lips, but she held back. The way he stared at her, she could see he shared her desire, but there was still something secretive and sorrowful lingering behind his dark eyes. Whatever it was kept her from giving in to her impulses. And it kept him from giving in to his.

He cleared his throat, breaking the spell. She glanced away nervously then lifted a small plate with a piece of chocolate cake and handed it to him.

"Let's eat this in the living room," he said.

"Sounds good. I'll get the forks."

Katja settled in on the chair opposite Micah, with her

dessert plate in her lap and her glass of wine on the end table beside her. "So tell me about New York City," she said. "I'd love to go there someday."

"Well, New York City is pretty spectacular, but my mother's family is actually from upstate New York. Lots of pastures and farms. Small towns, mining communities."

"When was the last time you were there?"

"Ten years ago when I was a gawky teen. My cousins teased me relentlessly about my accent and about my 'Euro' wardrobe."

"Sounds awful."

"It wasn't so bad. I spent the summer there, and by the end of it my accent was all but gone, and my mother had bought me a truck load of American-style clothes."

"How did your mother and father meet?"

"After my mother graduated from business college, she took a summer off to travel Europe with her then boyfriend. They spent time in Hamburg hanging out in student pubs, and that's where she met my father. They hit it off, and my mother dumped her boyfriend to be with my dad. They got married that next summer, and she's lived in Germany ever since."

"That's quite the love story."

"Yeah, I guess."

"I wonder why your dad didn't move to America. I know a lot of guys who'd jump at the chance. And New York is so exciting. Full of romance and possibilities."

Katja blushed when she realized she used the word "romance." Micah's eyes widened slightly, but then he graciously ignored it.

"Dad's career had already started here. My grandfather was also in banking, and even back then, it didn't hurt to have a leg up. I remember a time when Mama used to try to convince Papa to move to New York, but she's since given up, I think."

"There's still time," Katja said.

Micah shook his head. "She won't go if I don't go."

"Don't you want to go?"

The shadow that followed Micah around, settled over his features. He answered quietly. "I can't."

She wanted to know why. She desperately wanted to know what had Micah so bound and shackled. He'd almost opened up to her tonight and now, suddenly, he'd collapsed into himself again. She wanted to ask him, but his closed look frightened her. The wrong word would chase him away, and she wasn't willing to risk it.

"Feel like watching a movie?" she asked, hoping to lighten things up again.

Micah blinked, and she was sure he was going to decline and tell her he needed to go to bed, but instead he nodded. "Okay. It's your birthday. You choose."

Katja scrolled through the options, wondering if a romance would be okay, but then deciding against it. Better an action-adventure flick. She was about to suggest one when Micah's phone buzzed.

His expression widened with disbelief. He stared at Katja with something close to fear. "My mother just texted. She and my dad are in Dresden. They just parked the car and are on their way up."

HIS AMERICAN MOTHER

"Quick!" Micah blurted. "We have to move your stuff!"

Micah traveled through the living room gathering every object that would point to the fact that Katja was staying there. Her bag of clothes, the extra pillow and blanket: he traipsed to his room and tossed them behind the door. Katja stood there feeling flabbergasted at Micah's strange behavior. Had he not mentioned her even once in all the phone conversations he had with his mother? Was she a *secret*?

She snapped to attention and placed her guitar into its case and clicked it shut, then carried it along with her notebook and sketchpad and placed them on Micah's bed. She took a moment to look around. She'd peeked inside before but had never fully entered. He had a large, neatly made bed with a dark cover, a wood dresser and wardrobe and a brown throw rug that lay on the wood floor on the side of the bed Micah favored. There was nothing frivolous about the décor. It was thoroughly masculine.

Micah entered with an armful of her things she'd left in the bathroom. Her makeup bag and hair products. Her brush.

She waved her hands about. "What's the deal, Micah?"

"I'm sorry. It's just, my mother…"

They heard tapping on the door and Micah grabbed her arm, pulling her out of the room, closing his bedroom door tightly behind him. Katja was extremely perplexed by Micah's behavior. She'd never seen him lose his cool and unravel like this before.

"What should I do?" she said, feeling terrified now at the prospect of her imminent introduction to Micah's parents.

"Just stand there. It'll be fine."

His voice betrayed his own conviction, and she absolutely doubted that it would be fine.

"Mama! Papa!" Micah invited his parents in, and Katja was surprised by the physical affection that followed. Big hugs complete with kisses to both cheeks, along with verbal praises (his father's in German and his mother's in English) about how great Micah looked. They obviously loved him. Maybe too much.

They entered the kitchen area that opened up to the living room and stopped short when they spotted Katja standing there. She had her hands folded in front of her like a young girl scared of her teacher on her first day of school.

Micah's father was a handsome man for his age, with greying temples and the same warm, brown eyes as his son. His mother looked like Meryl Streep in, *The Devil Wears Prada*. She wore a high-end, fitted dress suit and four-inch stilettos, definitely brand name items. Her hair was short and blond and perfectly styled. She wore fashionable glasses, which she slowly removed as her eyes roamed from Katja's face, down to her feet and back again.

"Hello," Katja said timidly.

Frau Sturm looked at her son and said in English, "Seriously, Micah?"

79

He frowned and returned in English. "Now, don't be rude."

Katja took English all through school, and of course listened to a lot of English music and watched English movies. She wasn't that comfortable speaking it, but she understood a lot.

"Of course." She turned back to Katja and spoke once again in German. "Who is your friend?"

"Mama, Papa, this is Katja Stoltz."

Frau Sturm stepped close to Katja and offered her hand. Katja shook it, hating how her palms had suddenly grown damp. "Good day," Frau Sturm said stiffly.

Herr Sturm was slightly more cordial. He shook Katja's hand and smiled, "It's my pleasure to meet you." Then he settled on the chair nearest the window and stared outside.

Frau Strum continued, "So, Katja, how did you meet my son?"

Katja's face grew red at the memory of being picked up on the street like a common hooker. Her eyes flashed to Micah for help.

"I saw her playing at a pub. She's very good."

Frau Sturm's eyes darted to Micah and then back to Katja. "You're a musician?"

"Yes," Katja said. "And an artist." She didn't know why she added that. This woman just made her so nervous.

Frau Sturm's gaze landed on the wall behind her, to the three framed sketches. Her heels clicked along the floor as she walked over to examine them. "These are new, Micah," she stated.

Herr Sturm twisted to look, apparently amused by the dramatic scene playing out in front of him.

"I thought it time to hang something up," Micah muttered.

"*Hmm*," Frau Sturm hummed. She turned back to Katja. "Is this your signature?"

Katja nodded. She waited for a commentary on the quality of her work, but Frau Sturm's lips formed a firm line. Then she said, "What do you do for employment?"

"Mama?" Micah said, breathing out hard. "What's with the interrogation?"

"What?" Frau Sturm feigned puzzlement. "I'm just trying to get to know your friend."

"I work at the coffee shop around the corner," Katja blurted out. It was a lie. She didn't work anywhere, but she didn't want Frau Sturm to think she was an unemployed bum. She wasn't sure why she cared what this woman thought, but she did. And she did know why. She was Micah's mother, an important person to him, and she knew deep down she had the power to take him from her.

Even though he wasn't hers.

What was the matter with her? Katja couldn't remember the last time she'd felt so flustered and so... lacking.

Frau Sturm turned to Micah. "I must visit your bathroom."

It was like a tornado died down when Micah's mother disappeared behind the closed bathroom door.

Katja stared at Micah with wide eyes and whispered, "Should I leave?"

He shook his head sharply. "No."

Katja slumped into one of the chairs, feeling completely exhausted and depleted.

Herr Sturm's interest returned to something outside the window. "Are you planning on staying at this branch for a while, then?" he said without looking at his son.

Micah frowned. Katja sensed there was something

deeper implied by the question. Micah didn't answer. Instead he said, "I'll get us some drinks."

Katja knew he meant juice or water or tea, but she could use something much stronger right about now.

Frau Sturm came out in time to accept Micah's offer of a tall glass of sparkling water. She took it, then motioned for him to follow her into the kitchen.

Even though his mother made an attempt to lower her voice, Katja could easily hear her, and she understood her English perfectly. "What's going on here, Micah? The truth now."

"I don't know what you mean?"

"That girl. She looks like…"

"Mother!"

"Are you living together?"

"No, it's not like that."

"I found feminine items under the sink."

Oh, good Lord, Katja thought. She'd left a box of tampons there.

"You were snooping?" Micah's voice was hard and low. Katja could picture the look on his face. Narrowed eyes, deep lines pulling his lips into a frown.

"Don't deflect. This girl isn't right for you."

Katja stood sharply and grabbed her coat and purse. She couldn't avoid seeing Micah and his mother as she approached the door.

"I'm sorry, Micah. I forgot, I have this thing." She couldn't think of anything nice to say to his mother, so she said nothing. She did make a point of slamming the door when she left.

PARTY GIRL

NOT SURPRISINGLY, Katja found herself sitting on a bar stool at the Blue Note, her home away from home.

"Hello, *ma Cherie*," Maurice said when he saw her. "Oh, why the sad face?"

"It's my birthday," Katja said. "I need a drink."

"All the best! We must celebrate!" Maurice removed her favorite wine from the shelf and poured her a glass. It warmed her heart that he remembered the kind of wine she liked.

"So." He leaned thick elbows on the counter. "How old are we today?"

She took a long drink and then sighed. "*We* are twenty-one years old."

"Oh, yes. The twenties. Such an exciting time of one's life."

Katja didn't share his enthusiasm. "Can I ask you something, Maurice?"

"Sure."

"Why don't you live in France?"

He grinned coyly. "How can I live there, when my true love is here?"

His answer surprised her. "You're married?"

His smile faltered. "My dear wife passed away five

years ago. I joke that my bar is my true love now, but my heart knows better. I'm here in Dresden because it was the hometown of my beautiful wife, and it's my home now. We were married for twenty-five years." He winked. "Otherwise, the Blue Note *would* be in France."

Suddenly Renata's face flashed across Katja's mind. "Do you think you'll ever remarry?"

He washed a glass in a sink of soapy water. "I doubt it. I don't think love like that comes along twice in a lifetime." He smiled and put the glass he was drying on the shelf. "She was the sun to my moon."

Did he really say that? "The sun to your moon?"

"Yes, like your song."

A shrill ring came from Katja's purse on the counter.

"Your purse is ringing," Maurice said. He left her to serve other customers. Katja removed her new phone and stared at it. She didn't want to talk to Micah right now. She pushed ignore, switched it to vibrate and shoved it in her back pocket.

The front door of the pub opened continuously, and the place was soon full. Music pumped from the speakers in the corners and Katja started to relax in the party atmosphere. Sebastian and Karl-Heinz were there, and she sat in a chair across from them.

"Hey," she said. "It's my birthday."

"All the best!" Sebastian said. "Your next drink is on me."

Katja readily accepted it. She wanted to drink. She wanted to forget. "Thanks!" She looked around for Sebastian's girlfriend. "Where's Yvonne?"

Sebastian shrugged and ran a hand through his spiky hair. "She has some family thing."

Karl-Heinz leaned across the table. She observed him with her artist's eye. He had messy black hair and thick eyebrows. His eyes were a grey blue and he had slender lips. He'd be an interesting subject.

"Where's your boyfriend?" he said.

Katja squinted at him. "I don't have a boyfriend."

He flashed her a lopsided grin. "I think my night just got a whole lot better."

She laughed. He was flirting with her. See? She *was* desirable. Guys *did* like her. Take that, Micah Sturm. She winked at Karl-Heinz and slugged back her drink.

She liked the buzz. It made her happy. It made her feel good about herself. She didn't need anything or anyone. Especially not *him*.

Why did her butt keep vibrating? She reached back and found the phone. Oh yeah, her birthday gift from Micah.

"*Heelllooo*," she sang. "What? I can't hear you. Blue Note? Heck, yeah!" It took a couple tries to push the tiny end call button—why'd they make it so blurry anyway?

"Does anyone want to dance?" she shouted.

Karl-Heinz reached out a hand. "I'm game."

She swayed with the upbeat music, and Karl-Heinz pulled her close until her body slammed into his. His hands moved down her shoulders and over her hips. She pulled away a little, not exactly comfortable with how close they were, but at the same time it felt good. His hands on her body signaled to her that he wanted her. *She was wanted*.

She felt his lips brush her forehead, and she stiffened slightly. She didn't know him, but, she decided at that moment, she didn't care. She just wanted to be loved, and if *he* wouldn't love her, she'd take it from wherever she could get it.

Karl-Heinz whispered in her ear. "Do you want to get out of here?"

She knew what he was saying. Did she want to sleep

with him? No. Besides, she hadn't been here long, and she wanted to party.

She felt a hand on her shoulder before she could answer. She turned and burst out laughing. "Micah? What are *you* doing here?"

Why are you here?

I don't want you here.

I really want you here.

He didn't smile. He flashed Karl-Heinz a blistering glare, then said to her, "Let's go home."

She pulled away from both of them. "I don't want to go *home*. I don't *have* a home. I want to *paarrrttttyyy*."

Katja stumbled back to the table and squeezed in beside Sebastian. "You're such a good friend," she slurred. She picked up his drink and took a sip. "You don't try to use me. You don't try to change me. You're not ashamed of me."

Sebastian wrapped an arm around her shoulders and gently removed his drink from her with the other. "I think you've had too much to drink already."

"I don't care," she whined. "It's my birthday."

She was vaguely aware of the two empty seats in front of them becoming occupied by Karl-Heinz and Micah. They both looked frustrated. They both could go fly a kite.

"Sebastian," she said. "Why do we do this?"

"Do what?"

"This?" She flung out an arm almost knocking Sebastian's drink over. He expertly rescued it. "Play music. Write songs. What drives us to pursue this life so hard?"

"It's the way we're built, baby. Not playing is like not breathing."

Katja narrowed her gaze at Micah, but continued to converse with Sebastian. "He doesn't approve," she slurred. "His family are *bankers*. They don't get people like *us*."

Katja was drunk, but not so much that she didn't catch the hurt that flashed in Micah's eyes. He shifted as if to leave, but she reached across the table and grabbed his wrist.

"Don't go. I'm sorry." She pulled a sad, pleading puppy dog face. "Please."

She giggled when Micah relaxed back in his chair. "Micah doesn't drink," she announced. She raised her half-empty glass. "Can you believe it? He's my designated driver. Except that we walked here. He's my designated walker!" She lifted her drink to her lips and emptied it.

She slammed her glass down and locked eyes with Micah. "I want to dance. With you."

He slowly reached his hand out and lifted her to the dance floor. She leaned into him and swayed with the music. It was so different than with Karl-Heinz. He held her gently, stroking her hair. He didn't grope her like she was a play thing. She wondered why.

She looked up at him, and soaked in his beautiful, brown eyes. "Are you gay?"

His eyebrows jumped. "No."

"Have you ever had a girlfriend?"

Micah swallowed. "Yes."

"Do you know what Maurice told me?"

"Uh, nope."

"His wife was the sun to his *moon*. He said that. She's dead now, but *she* was the sun to his moon. Isn't that romantic? He said he got that from my *song*."

Micah laughed a little. "It's a great song."

"So, why don't you like me?"

His eyes grew sad again. "I do like you, Katja. Very much. But you've been drinking, and you're probably not going to like having this conversation now. Let's save it until later, okay?"

"Okay." Katja rested her head against his chest. Micah was such a nice guy. Such a good, decent, nice guy. His prissy, judgmental mother was right about her, though. She wasn't good enough for her son.

THE HANGOVER

KATJA WOKE up the next morning on the sofa bed in Micah's living room with a splitting headache and no recollection of how she got there. She still wore the clothes she had on the day before, so Micah obviously hadn't felt comfortable stripping her and putting her into her night T-shirt. She was glad of it. She already had far too much to be mortified over.

Her jeans cut into her knees and her stomach. She eased the top button open to relieve the pressure. The room swirled when she attempted to sit up. She had to go to the bathroom. And she thought she might throw up.

It was too much to hope for that she would've forgotten the night before. No, she remembered everything. Every shameful thing. Her sensual dance with Karl-Heinz, the horrible things she said about Micah right in front of him. Her questions and confessions.

Ugh.

And then there was the whole fiasco before it with his *über*-domineering mother. The anger she felt at Micah for making her pretend she didn't live here, like she was a dirty little secret, bubbled up again.

She should move out. She knew this, but where to go? There had to be some place.

Karl-Heinz would probably make room for a new roommate.

The thought made her gag.

Her eyes traced the wall where her sketches hung, and the memory of Frau Sturm's body bending forward to scrutinize her work, burned in her mind. Then she noticed the locked door. Her sun and moon sketch was missing.

A deep sadness streamed through her.

She forced herself to get up and made it to the bathroom without puking on the floor or wetting her pants. Her next stop was the kitchen, where she drank a half a bottle of juice straight from the container, popped two aspirin, then prepared a strong coffee.

Micah had placed her duffle bag along with her guitar and notebooks in the hall outside his bedroom door. She plucked out a clean shirt, underwear and jeans and headed for the shower. She let the hot water pour down on her head for a good while.

Afterward, she put the sofa bed back into its sofa form and by then she could face a little breakfast. Her eyes continued to dart to the blank space on the locked room door, and she wondered why Micah took it down. Did his mother have something to do with it?

She cringed at the memory of the questions she asked Micah at the Blue Note, especially when she asked him if he'd ever had a girlfriend. Of course a guy like that would've had a girlfriend before. Likely a lot of girlfriends. Ugh, how infantile could she get?

He probably wanted her out, and she didn't blame him. If she owned a laptop, she'd check the want ads right now. As it were, she'd have to read the papers. They carried local ones at the coffee shop.

As usual, Katja took her sketch pad with her. Her favorite table was empty and since she just ate and drank a coffee, she didn't bother to stand in line. She sat down and started sketching. Her hand moved as if of its own free will. Another face. This one wasn't a patron in the shop. This was a face she knew from memory. Dark, moody eyes, a narrow nose. A square jaw, with full lips in a near frown. Hair trimmed short but growing out around small ears. Behind him, a shadow. She didn't know what it was. A ghost of his past. Some trauma that left an echo.

She jumped when the chair in front of her moved. Renata sat down and looked at her with questioning eyes.

"Is everything all right? You look pensive."

She was about to say everything was fine, but something in her burned to tell someone her problems. She didn't have any real friends besides Renata.

"I'm alone."

"What do you mean? You must have family?"

Katja shook her head sadly. "Not really. It's a long story."

"What about that boy I see you walking around with sometimes."

"I don't think he's interested."

Renata cupped her hand with hers. "*Schätzchen*, you are never alone. God is always there for you."

Katja smiled. Renata was such a kind hearted lady, but she obviously never had any real problems in her life.

Renata saw the look of doubt on her face. "My husband left me ten years ago. I raised our two children alone, all the while working here day and night. I've had my share of problems, but I'm all right. And you'll be all right, too. So tell me what you need."

Katja felt appropriately chastised, but at the same time accepted. Renata was a person she could trust.

"I need to move, and I don't have any money. Actually," Katja's gaze darted to the newspaper stand by the counter. "I should be reading the papers, looking for a job."

"Why don't you work here? One of our employees just quit yesterday, and you know how busy it can get in the afternoons."

"You mean right now?"

"Yes. I can teach you everything you need to know in an hour."

"Don't I have to talk to the boss?"

Renata laughed. "I am the boss."

By the time the afternoon rush hit, Katja was versed in all methods of coffee making: cappuccinos, macchiato, espressos, lattes and plain old coffee. She knew all the kind of teas they offered and how to present the pastries. She'd even mastered the till.

What surprised her most was how much she enjoyed the work. She liked interacting with the customers, working alongside the other employees, especially Renata, and she even enjoyed cleaning off the tables.

Before she knew it, it was well past six o'clock, well past the time Micah would be home from work and wondering what had happened to her. She checked her phone and noticed several missed calls.

She went to the back of the restaurant to call back.

"Hey," he said. "Just wondering where you are. If you're okay."

"Actually, I'm at work."

"Work?"

She smiled at the surprise in his voice. "Yeah. I'm working at the café."

"Right, you kind of mentioned you got a job."

It wasn't true at the time, but it was now. Katja didn't see the need to point that out.

"Yeah, so I'm not sure when I'll be done here."

"That's fine. I was just worried that maybe you left, or something."

"Micah, did you not see my guitar in the hallway?"

He chuckled. "Right. Okay. See you soon."

When Katja got back to Micah's flat, he had leftovers waiting for her. She didn't think she was hungry until she saw them and set to work putting them in the microwave.

"How was your day?" Micah said from his spot on the sofa. It was a reversal of roles. She was normally the one who asked him that.

"Good. I like working there. Renata, my boss, is great."

She didn't want to get into details like she would if he weren't someone she was trying to figure out. What role exactly did Micah play in her life anyway? Roommate? Friend? More than friend, but not quite boyfriend?

A better question was what role did she play in his life? Roommate? Friend? More than friend, but not yet girl-friend? Moocher he wished would just move out already?

His expression was unreadable. Her eyes moved to the blank space on the locked door and his gaze followed hers. He looked at the floor and then his hands and finally back to her face.

The microwave pinged, and she brought her hot plate to the table. Her appetite had disappeared in the twenty minutes she'd been back. She played with her food. "I can look for my own place now that I have a job."

Micah moved from the living room to the chair oppo-site her in the kitchen. "I want to apologize for yesterday. For my mother's rudeness, but especially for the uncom-fortable position I put you in. I should've just told her the way things are here."

"Why didn't you?"

"Did you see her? She's scary!" His eyes glinted with

humor, but Katja could tell there was a hint of truth there. She held back her smile.

"Katja, I understand if you want to go. I do. But I want you to know, that I don't want you to."

"What do you want?"

"I… can't say."

"What does that mean? Why can't you say? Why do you have to be such a mystery all the time?" Katja dropped her fork on her plate with a clang. "You're like a puzzle with too many missing pieces."

Micah inhaled and let his head flop back. Then he looked at her. "I know. That's all I can give you right now. I'm sorry."

He left her alone to finish her meal. When she heard his bedroom door click shut, she got up and scraped her dinner into the garbage. She held back the dam of tears that threatened to burst, and burned through her frustration by aggressively doing the dishes and cleaning the kitchen.

She got herself ready for bed, pulled out the sofa bed and draped the blanket over her body. She twisted and turned. There was no way sleep would come. She stared at the ceiling with her hands behind her head. Her eyes had adjusted to the dark and her gaze moved to the wall, landing on the empty spot on the locked door.

She remembered the sketch she drew of Micah. What would he say if he spotted it hanging there, in place of the sun and moon? Katja's rebellious streak was roused. She opened her sketch pad and ripped out the etching. She fished the scotch tape out of her bag and stepped quietly down the hall. She folded the tape and pressed the paper to the door.

She stepped back to take a look, then frowned. Maybe this wasn't a great idea. Maybe he'd think she was being passive aggressive or something. Or maybe he'd like the fact she bothered to sketch him. Or at least he'd be intrigued. Maybe he'd be creeped out?

She placed one hand on the knob as the other hovered over the sketch in indecision. Leave it or take it down? She shifted her weight and her hand pressed down on the handle. It moved and Katja heard a click.

The door opened.

THE STORY

She flicked on the light.

It was a small room, unfurnished except for a wooden desk pushed up against the back wall. A gold-plated reading lamp was aimed at a large cork board hanging above it. On it was a map of Germany along with several pictures of young women, all with long, honey-blond hair similar to Katja's.

She swallowed hard, a thread of fear shivering up her spine.

White plastic thumb tacks were pressed into different cities and towns and red wool was stretched between them like a bloody spider's web. What *was* this? Who were these girls? Were they... victims? Were they... *dead*?

Who was Micah Sturm? The glaring fact was she didn't know the guy at all. She'd trusted a stranger blindly, and she might just pay for her gullibility with her life. Every survival instinct kicked into gear. She had to get out of there. Now.

"You weren't supposed to see this."

Katja jumped at his voice. He stood in the doorway, bare-chested in boxer shorts, arms hanging loosely by his side. His hair was messed in the way she normally found attractive. His expression was sad.

She felt something she'd never felt before in his presence. Fear. Her chest tightened and her nerves tingled up and down her arms and legs. She was naked except for her underwear and the long sleeping T-shirt she wore. She felt vulnerable and exposed, trapped by someone whom she now suspected was mad and possibly dangerous. She folded her bare arms across her chest in a feigned attempt to look tough and unafraid. "Who are these girls?"

Micah took a step forward; she took an immediate step back. The expression on his face darkened.

"It's only one girl," he said. "Why are you afraid of me?"

Katja flashed him a startled look. *Maybe because you're crazy?* A *stalker*? Katja's mind raced. Was Micah a killer? Did he have a fetish for girls with light-colored eyes and honey-blond hair? Girls like *her*? Was she to be his next picture tacked to the wall? Maybe this was the real reason why his mother had acted so possessively. Maybe she didn't hate Katja. Maybe she feared for her life!

"I'm not afraid." Her voice trembled, betraying her lie. "Just let me go."

Micah stepped away from the door. "You're free to leave any time."

Katja sprinted past him. She wished he didn't watch her as she struggled into her jeans, pulling them up over bare legs. She pushed all her belongings into her duffle bag. She placed her guitar in its case and closed it, snapping the fasteners. She grabbed her coat.

"Won't you at least let me explain?" Micah asked, softly.

Katja hesitated. Did she want to know?

She risked a glance, and her heart softened at the grief in his eyes. The pain there made her chest squeeze. These weren't the eyes of a killer. Something else was going on.

"Okay," she said. She owed him that much. He'd rescued her from the streets, taking her in like a stray kitten, no questions asked. Maybe his kindness was a result of something other than a snare. A snare he hadn't yet snapped.

She sat on the kitchen chair closest to the door, her things by her feet. If he made a move, she'd at least be able to reach the door to the stairwell and scream.

He disappeared for a moment, then reappeared wearing jeans and a button down shirt left open. He walked carefully to the chair opposite Katja and sat down.

"The girl in the photos is Greta. She's my girlfriend." He ran his hands through his hair and squeezed his eyes shut. "Or was. Was my girlfriend."

Katja watched as a flurry of emotions crossed Micah's face. "What happened?"

"Three years ago we were at a party. We partied a lot back then, and I was one of the wild ones."

Katja found that hard to believe but stayed quiet.

"I drank too much, dabbled in drugs. Always after the good time. Greta was worried about me, wanted me to slow down, but I just laughed it off. Laughed at her."

"And?" Katja prompted.

"We went to another party. Greta didn't want to go, but I coerced her. I was good at manipulating people and always managed to get my way, especially with her. Someone gave me something, pills, I don't know what they were. They hit me hard and I passed out. The last thing I remember is stretching out on a sofa with my arms around Greta. When I came to, she was gone."

"She left the party without you?"

"That's what I thought. I was angry, but I didn't blame her. I went home, showered, got myself together and started calling her. She didn't answer her phone. I figured she must be really mad at me for getting so wasted. I wanted to explain to her that it wasn't my fault. I got bad junk."

He sighed long and hard. "Of course it was my fault for being willing to take anything at all."

"So, I'm guessing she broke up with you?" Katja said. This was the part that made her nervous. Micah was a guy obsessed with a girl who obviously wanted out of the relationship.

He stared out the window and then back at Katja. "No. I wish it were that simple. I went to her house and no one knew where she was. Her parents thought she was with me, and when I assured them she wasn't, we became frantic. We called all her friends, everyone she knew, searched the places she liked to hang out. Finally, her parents called the police."

Katja's heart pounded. She gripped her thighs and dug her fingernails in. "Where was she?"

Micah shook his head. "We never found her. She's been missing for three years."

Katja's breath hitched. "*Missing*?"

"The authorities immediately suspected me." He rubbed his face. "It was awful. I was desperate to find her and instead of being out there looking, I was held up in a jail cell. The fact that I was passed out all night with several witnesses secured my alibi. I'd lost a few days, but I made it my mission to find her. I followed every lead, every tip. I set up a website, a Facebook page, but nothing. It was like she'd disappeared off the face of the earth."

His gaze moved from his hands to Katja's face. His eyes were so full of pain, Katja's own heart ached.

"She was my first serious girlfriend." Micah's voice cracked. "I would've married her."

His shoulders shook as he gave into weeping. His chin

dropped to his chest, and his hair hung over his forehead. Katja felt hot tears pool behind her eyes. She wanted to go to him, comfort him, but she was immobile.

Micah tugged the cuff of his shirt sleeve and wiped his eyes. "Sometimes I get an anonymous tip that someone thinks they spotted her in this town or that one. It's why I move around so much. I'm always looking for her."

It made sense to Katja now. "You thought I was her, the night you stopped to pick me up."

"Yes."

"How long are you going to keep looking for her?"

"I don't know."

Statistically Katja knew that a young woman who'd been missing for three years was probably dead. By the stricken look on Micah's face, she believed he knew that, too.

"I'm sorry," she said.

Micah shrugged. "It's my fault."

"How is it your fault?"

"If I hadn't passed out, I would've taken her home. She would be safe. She would be…"

Alive.

Micah stood, keeping his eyes on Katja. "I don't want you to go, but you already know that. I understand if you need to leave. You're welcome to stay if you change your mind."

He walked to his room and closed his door.

Katja dragged her things back to the living room. She'd changed her mind a long time ago.

LETTING GO

Katja awoke once again to the aroma of fresh coffee. Her eyes flickered open, adjusting to the light. Judging by the brightness in the room, she'd slept in.

Then the events of the previous night exploded in her memory and her eyes widened. She sprung to a sitting position and searched the apartment.

For him.

He was sitting at the kitchen table, coffee cup in hand, staring at her. Had he been watching her sleep?

"Why are you home?" she asked when their eyes met.

"It's Saturday." He lifted his cup. "Coffee?"

He was freshly showered, hair slicked back with the odd curl escaping to his forehead and his face shaved. He wore the same shirt he'd pulled on in a hurry the night before but it was buttoned closed now. His expression was different: lighter, friendlier. His lips actually pulled up in a slight smile.

He looked good.

Katja suddenly felt self-conscious, knowing how she always had crazy bedhead in the morning and probably also had wrinkle imprints on her cheek from her pillow case.

"Uh, sure. I just need to…" She waved to the bathroom. She pulled her long T down over her butt before standing and moved rapidly. A quick glance in the mirror confirmed her fears. She looked a mess.

She washed her face and brushed her hair, clipping it back with two barrettes. She heard the espresso machine wail and smiled a little. Micah was making one just for her.

She put on her jeans and a shirt, and at the last moment a little mascara and lip gloss.

Her coffee was waiting for her when she returned, but Micah was nowhere. She fought back her disappointment. She took her cup to the window and stared out as she drank. It was a sunny morning, and the park that ran along the river was full of sun seekers, walking and cycling.

"Would you like to go out?"

She startled at Micah's voice. *Go out?*

"We could eat breakfast in the park."

Katja nodded. "That sounds great."

Micah already had buns with meat and cheese made up by the time Katja finished her coffee. He tossed a couple apples into the bag and grabbed two bottles of water.

Katja smiled. A picnic.

She slipped into a coat and followed Micah down the stairs and outside. The warmth of the sun on her face was a balm to her soul. She didn't mind that she still needed a light jacket, so long as she could wear her sunglasses as well. They chose a spot on the grass across the river from the magnificent baroque Semper Opera House.

Micah spread out a blanket and set the bag of food in the middle. Katja sat across from him and smiled broadly as he handed her half of the meal. They ate in silence, people watching. Katja couldn't stop herself from sneaking glances at Micah, thankful for the sunglasses that hid her eyes. He brushed the crumbs off his hands and then rested his arms on his knees.

He cleared his throat. "About last night…"

"It's okay," Katja broke in. "You don't have to talk about it."

"I want to if it's okay with you. I feel like I need to talk to someone about it."

Katja was willing to listen. "Okay." She put her uneaten food away and sipped from her water bottle.

Micah rubbed his face. "I don't know where to start."

"Would it help if I asked you questions?"

His eyes cut to hers. "Ask me anything."

"Where did you grow up?"

"Hamburg."

"That's where you met?"

Micah nodded. "We went to school together."

She knew the story up to Greta's disappearance. She wanted to know what happened afterward. With Micah.

"You said you've been following tips, moving around the country trying to find her. How many times have you moved in the last three years?"

"Nine."

Nine. Wow.

"Where were you before Dresden?"

"Stuttgart."

Katja was confused. Micah obviously had money. "How does that work with your job?"

"My father is a board member of the bank I work for. He pulls strings to get me a new position every time I move."

"He must believe in your mission?"

Micah shook his head and blew out a breath. "No, but he believes in me. Or at least in helping me. I'm grateful for his support, but I know he'd be the first to cheer if I told him I was stopping the quest."

Micah lay flat on his back, folding his arms over his lean chest. "My mother is another matter. She'd love for me to forget about my mission completely, and get on with my life." He chuckled humorlessly. "She doesn't think any girl is worth this much grief."

Katja remembered what Frau Sturm started to say. *She looks like...*

"Do we look a lot alike?" The question came out in a whisper. She'd seen the pictures of Greta, but it had to be more than hair and eyes.

Micah rolled onto his side, leaned on his elbow and stared at her.

"You do, but not exactly, of course."

Katja didn't understand the emotions that warred within her. She felt strangely *jealous*. She wanted to know who Micah thought was *prettier*. Could she be any shallower?

Micah continued, "Personality-wise, you're very different."

That piqued Katja's interest. "How so?"

"Even though you're both outgoing and like to laugh, you are more introspective and conscientious. You care what people think, even if you don't want to. Greta is..."

Katja noticed that Micah talked about Greta in present tense, like he really believed she was still alive. She filled in the blank. "More self-confident?"

"She had an air about her, like she knew she was special. She didn't like to do things the way everyone else did. She wasn't the nicest person, really, but then again, neither was I." He cringed. "We were perfect for each other that way. Though," he added after a moment. "I think she was growing bored of me. I couldn't blame her for that."

He lay back and pinched his eyes shut. He looked broken and vulnerable. Katja felt her heart reaching for him, wanting to comfort him, wanting *him*, and she knew it was a dangerous place for her.

Even if he returned the feelings Katja was developing for him, how could she know she wouldn't just be a facsimile for Greta? A stand in?

She looked away and fought the heaviness building in her chest. She didn't know what else to say to him. She didn't have any more questions.

"I know it's time to let go," Micah finally said. "And I want to. I just don't know how."

Katja considered him. "Maybe you need to perform some kind of ceremony."

"Like a funeral?"

"Do you think she's dead?"

"For the longest time, I didn't. Greta was just too strong-willed to let someone else take her life. I know it sounds stupid." He sighed. "But now, after all this time, I don't know. If she were alive, she would've let someone know by now. She was selfish, but not that selfish."

"How about a memorial? Then you don't have to decide on her fate. She's just gone. Maybe saying goodbye in an official manner will help you to gain closure."

Micah flopped back and stared up at the clouds rolling across the sky. Katja watched the emotions race across his face: fear, sadness, regret.

"I don't know if I can do that," he said. He reached into his pocket, pulling out a pair of sunglasses, and put them on.

He didn't want her to see his struggle. He was shutting her out.

That was fine with Katja. She had no right to Micah or to know what was going on in his head. He said he was ready to let go, but obviously he wasn't.

Maybe she should leave? For real, this time. This thing with Micah was getting so complicated.

But then again, where would she go? She'd have to figure that out first. And she'd need more money than she had right now. She'd go talk to Maurice later today, see if she could book another gig. And there were other places in town. With her job at the café, she should be able to get her own place, or at least find a new roommate.

How many times had she had this exact thought? What was it about Micah that she just couldn't seem to leave him? But she would this time. Once she had enough money she'd head to Munich. She'd heard it was a good place for artists.

Micah removed his glasses and squinted at her. "What are you thinking about?"

"Nothing," Katja lied.

"Please don't leave."

Katja stared at him. Could he read her mind now? "Why not?"

"I'll do it. I'll do the ceremony. Just don't leave me."

After all he'd done for her, the least she could do was support him through this, right? Just a little more time. Then she'd go. For sure.

THE CEREMONY

KATJA STOOD in front of the locked door and waved Micah over. "We need to start here."

"What do you mean?"

"Your shrine. It has to go."

Micah looked stricken, frozen to the spot. Katja sighed. If he couldn't even tear down the cork board, how would he ever get through a ceremony? Her heart sank. He was in so deep, she doubted he'd ever get out.

Her shoulders collapsed as she let out a defeated breath.

Then Micah said, "I'll get the key."

She stepped aside as he opened the door.

Shivers ran up her spine as she stared at the board on the back wall. At Greta's pictures. Some of them were of her smiling and laughing, others showed her in serious thought. A search through the drawers found more photos of Greta and Micah together when they were happy.

Or seemingly happy.

Micah moved stiffly, like a robot, pulling out tacks, returning them to the box they'd come from. He piled the photos onto the desk, gently, pausing to stroke the odd one before reluctantly releasing it. All the newspaper clippings reporting on Greta's disappearance were stacked beside the photos in two neat piles. He rolled the red strands of wool into a clump.

He turned to Katja. "What should I do with this?"

"Burn it," she said without hesitation.

"*Burn* it?"

"If you really want to let go, you have to *let go*."

She picked up the photos and the papers, grabbing the yarn at the last minute, and headed to the kitchen. She dropped the items into the stainless steel sink, fished through a drawer and produced a lighter. She handed it to Micah. "You do it." She knew it was merely a symbolic gesture, that Micah had digital copies of all these photos somewhere, but it was an important step.

Micah slowly reached for it. His gaze moved from the lighter to the items in the sink. His hand shook when he lit the corner of the photo on top. He clamped his jaw tight, his expression pushing against a swirl of emotion.

Katja stood beside him as they watched Greta's face on the top photo gradually disappear behind a retreating black edge. Slowly the heat enveloped the pile until flames jumped out of the sink, and then the flames receded until the fire died, leaving the basin full of ashes.

Katja studied Micah, seeing his Adam's apple bob as he swallowed hard. "You can cry if you want to," she said.

He shook his head. "I'm done crying for her."

Katja fished through the cupboards until she found an empty jar under the sink, and handed it to him. "Put the ashes in here."

He hesitated, then wiped the inside of the sink with his palms, scooping up the ashes and letting them go into the jar Katja held for him. It took five swipes of the sink to fill it, and when the ashes reached the rim, Katja put the jar down on the table. She returned to turn on the tap, then reached for Micah's ash covered hands and held them under the stream of warm water. She washed them gently with soap, running her fingers between each of his, taking her time, caressing the tops of his hand and stroking his palms until every sign of ash was gone. It was strangely intimate and Katja felt a blush rush up her neck.

Micah's eyes washed over her as she took a towel and dried their hands. "Now what?" he said with a husky voice. The way he looked at her, with such affection and... adoration, yes, *adoration*, made her tremble.

She struggled with her own voice. "Let's go to the bridge."

Katja grabbed their jackets off the hooks and handed Micah's to him. She threaded her arms into hers and wondered as she watched him stand there unmoving, if she was going to have to dress him. Something clicked for him as she buttoned up her coat, and he finally shrugged his on.

She twisted the cap of the jar tightly, then handed it to Micah. This was his goodbye affair. He needed to carry it.

The sky was overcast and grey with a cool wind blowing from the north. Katja stuffed her hands in her pockets and kept stride with Micah. He held the jar with both hands close to his chest. The expression on his face was somber, and Katja hoped they were doing the right thing, that this exercise wasn't about to push him over some sharp, psychological edge.

They continued walking side by side without talking. The light at the highway was green when they got to the crossing so they didn't have to break stride. The stone bridge had just a few pedestrians crossing, and they soon came to an empty cut out, the same one Katja often busked in. They leaned over the thick, flat stone edge and spent a few moments looking down at the meandering water that flowed below. A boat lightly occupied with spring tourists motored underneath. Ducks and geese swam near the shoreline, their bottoms bouncing up into the air as they captured their meals. The river's song was soothing and melodic, perfect for what they were about to do.

Micah set the jar on the ledge and twisted off the cap.

"I'm sorry I lost you," he whispered. He gently turned the jar upside down and watched the ash disappear into the wind. "I'll see you in Heaven some day, Greta, but until then, goodbye."

Katja studied his face as he registered his loss. The ashes were gone. Greta was gone. He blinked a few times and exhaled. Then she saw something she rarely saw on Micah's face. *Relief.*

They stood there in silence for a few moments longer. Katja wondered if Micah had truly turned a corner. If *they* had turned a corner. She wrapped her arms tightly around herself in response to the spring chill, but the sun felt good. She lifted her sunglasses onto the top of her head and let the rays massage her face. She heard Micah take a long breath and slowly release it.

"Are you ready to go home?" she asked, swiping at strands of wind-blown hair and tucking them behind her ear.

He nodded lightly. "Yeah. And Katja?" He reached for her hand, threading his fingers through hers. She glanced at their joined palms feeling surprised, but pleased.

"Yes?"

His eyes grew warm as he took her in. "Thank you."

PRETTY WOMAN

WHEN THE FIRST of June rolled around, Katja insisted she start paying her half of the rent. Again, Micah refused it. She compromised by using only her own money to buy the groceries, which worked out better for her, since the rent on a flat this nice would be out of her budget anyway, even if she paid only half.

Micah's mood had improved dramatically since "the ceremony," and Katja hoped that maybe he could actually get over Greta after all.

They continued to spend evenings together, walking around *Neustadt* taking in live music, or staying home watching TV. One evening *Pretty Woman*, the 1990s movie starring Julia Roberts and Richard Gere, came on. Katja opened a bag of chips and poured them each a glass of Coke for the occasion.

"This is such a great movie," she said.

Micah wrinkled his brow. "Isn't it about a prostitute who falls in love with a rich guy?"

Katja nearly choked on a chip. She washed it down with the cola, and the bubbles burned up her nose. She coughed.

"Are you okay?" Micah asked.

"The rich guy fell in love with the prostitute." She

collapsed on the opposite end of the sofa, her face burning. Was that how Micah saw her? Did he still see her as a prostitute? Even though she never even *did* anything?

She felt his eyes sear her. She covered her face. She wanted to run and hide.

"Would you have?" Micah asked. Again, it was like he could read her mind. "If I'd paid you?"

He'd forgotten that he *had* paid her. He just didn't get anything for his money.

"What does it matter now?" she snapped.

He persisted. "But would you have?"

"Yes!" She glared at him. "Are you happy? You have no idea what it's like to be starving and cold and alone." She fought back tears. "It's just sex."

She felt the sofa shimmy as Micah moved closer. He traced her chin with his finger, forcing her to look at him. She shivered at his touch. "It's never just sex, Katja," he said. "Not with me."

Katja pinched her eyes shut and turned away. She wished she hadn't gone out that night. If it hadn't been for Irma…. but no, she couldn't blame her. She could only blame her own weakness. She was no better than any of those girls on the street.

She sighed. "What do you want from me?"

He inched closer. "I want you to know how valuable you are." He slid to the floor in front of her, forcing her to look at him. "Your body, your mind, your spirit. You are important, all of you, and… priceless. Don't sell yourself short, Katja. There's not enough money in the world that could buy you. Only love."

Her throat grew so dry, she could barely swallow. Where was this coming from? Why did he even care about her at all?

Micah sat back on the sofa beside her, so close they

were touching. His legs pressed against hers. He wrapped his arm around her shoulders and kissed her gently on the forehead.

It was the first time he'd shown her any kind of physical affection. The first time his lips touched her skin. She relished the pleasure it brought her.

"Okay," he said. "Let's watch this movie."

Katja bit her lip, fighting against the electricity his closeness had triggered. "I don't think we should." It came out in a husky moan. She winced.

Micah's eyebrows jumped. "We don't want to watch these two beautiful people fall in love?"

"No," Katja said adamantly. If she watched Edward and Vivian go at it on screen there'd be no stopping her from attacking Micah right there on the sofa. He'd warmed up to her, but he wasn't ready for that.

"There's another one on, where people shoot aliens and drive space ships," she said, reaching for the remote.

"Ah, I agree. Probably a better choice." Micah grinned. "For tonight, anyway."

HOW DEEP CAN YOU FEEL

WHEN KATJA STARTED WORKING at the café, Renata had requested she wear black dress pants and a white shirt under the coffee shop-issued apron, and she'd found just what she needed at the second hand shop. She discovered, of course, that she needed more than one set, so had been back since to buy more. She selected a clean set, got dressed and ready and now found that she still had an hour to burn before her shift began.

Katja collected her guitar, warmed up her fingers on a blues scale, then opened up her notebook. An idea had been percolating, and she scribbled out some lyrics.

It's all in how you look at it,
she said
As if there were a hundred ways to walk a high wire
Go on and try to let it go
Close your eyes and
Let your heart rule your head sometimes
How deep can you feel?

Yes, this was about Micah. All her lyric ideas were about Micah these days. And her mass of mixed-up emotions concerning him. Why did she steer him away last night? He wanted to watch a sappy romance with her, and she pushed for the dry, science-fiction flick. Did she want to be more than friends with Micah or not? She accused him of holding back, but she was equally to blame.

Deep down she knew the truth. She wasn't worthy of him. He might not know it yet, but he'd figure it out one day, and then he'd send her packing. For sure. A flare of anguish shot through her being at that thought. How would she cope with the real thing, when the imagined scenario caused so much pain?

She jotted down a few more lines and worked on some new melodies. Time passed quickly, and before she knew it, an hour was up already. She tossed her notepad aside, grabbed what she needed for work and rushed to get out the door.

Living around the corner from her workplace, Katja thought, should make it easier to get there on time, but she found it almost made it worse. The problem was the false sense that she could get there in thirty seconds, when you really need five full minutes.

She dashed down the stairs, pushed through the door to the outside and raced to the corner. She panicked a little when the little man light flashed red indicating she had to wait at the intersection, but fortunately he turned green shortly after. Katja didn't think Renata would be mad if she were a few seconds late, but she had been kind enough to give Katja a chance at this job, and she didn't want to appear ungrateful or like she took it for granted.

"Hello, Katja!" Renata said, greeting her when she blew in.

"Hi, Renata. I hope I'm not late."

Renata glanced up at the big clock on the wall. The minute hand was one minute past the hour. She grinned. "I bet you were lost in a new song."

Katja put her apron on. "I was. How did you know?"

Renata waved a hand. "My son's an artist. I'm aware of how the creative mind works. Or doesn't work."

Katja cleaned the coffee machine, wiped down tables after patrons left and tidied up the displays. When the mid-afternoon rush began she helped Renata take orders, making gourmet drinks and providing sweet treats before exchanging cash. Occasionally, customers came in just wanting a selection of buns or a loaf of bread. Katja would put on her plastic gloves to remove them from the display and place them into paper takeaway bags.

A guy with a boyish face and neatly parted hair arrived during a lull. "Hello," he said. "You must be Katja. My mother speaks very highly of you."

His mother? "Oh, you must be Renata's son," she said, smiling.

He smiled back and held out a hand. "I'm Jonas." Katja shook his hand, noticing the splattering of paint speckles on his arm. This was the artist.

Renata called his name when she spotted him, and he made his way around the counter to the back of the store. Katja watched as mother and son gave each other an affectionate embrace.

Jonas told Renata about an art fair he was invited to show at. Renata beamed and gave him another hug. Something twisted in Katja's heart as she watched. Renata was a good mother. How different Katja's life would be if her own mother had been as aware of her as Renata was of her children. If only her own mother had offered her support as she followed her dreams.

"Katja."

Katja snapped out of her reverie when Renata called her. "Yes?"

"Jonas is exhibiting his art at a festival here in Neustadt next month," she boasted.

"That's great," Katja offered sincerely. She understood how hard it was to make it as an artist, no matter the art form.

"Katja's an artist, too," Renata said to her son. "She's very good." Katja felt herself blush. So that was what it would feel like to have a parent who was proud of you.

"And she's a great singer-songwriter, too," Renata went on.

"Renata, please."

"No, it's true."

"Actually," Jonas started, "the organizer is looking for someone to play acoustic music in the background. You play guitar, right?"

Katja nodded.

"I could give you his contact info if you like."

"Really?"

"Yeah. I don't know what the pay's like…"

"Anything would be great."

Jonas took a napkin and jotted down the information. Katja slipped it into her pocket. "Thanks." Another paying gig, no matter how small, or how far in the background she'd be, was great.

Jonas said goodbye and waved as he left. Renata called out, Mach's gut, Schatz! Take care, treasure, not caring who heard. Jonas waved.

Katja was happy that Renata was obviously so close to her son, but she couldn't help feeling a sense of loss for herself. This was what she'd missed out on.

Thankfully, the shop got busy again, forcing Katja to push the lingering sadness away. The line was suddenly long, and she just focused on each customer as they reached the counter.

"May I help you?" she offered the next man without looking first. When she glanced up she gasped at the hand-some, familiar face. "Micah? What are you doing here?"

His eyes twinkled. "I think I'm getting a coffee."

Katja tilted her head. "You have a perfectly good coffee maker at home."

"Ah, yes," he admitted slowly, "but I don't have a Berliner donut." He watched her and his mouth twitched. "Or you, to serve it to me."

Katja gaped. Was Micah Sturm flirting with her? "Well, in that case, allow me."

As quickly as the crowd had assembled, it disappeared, leaving Katja alone with Micah at the counter and Renata hovering behind. She approached with a friendly grin.

"Oh," Katja said, seeing her. "This is my friend and my boss, Frau Renata Beck. And this is…" She opted for no description. "…Micah."

"Nice to meet you," Micah said, reaching to shake Renata's hand.

"Likewise." Renata let her eyebrows jump when Micah had looked away, indicating to Katja that she approved. She smirked and left to busy herself at the back.

Katja resumed with Micah's order, thankful that

Renata hadn't said anything to embarrass her. "Will that be to stay or to go?"

"Sadly, I must get back to work, so please make it to go."

Katja made his coffee and poured it into a takeaway cup. She used the tongs to place the crème-filled, chocolate-glazed donut in a small paper bag.

"So, I'm curious," she said as she waited for him to dig the proper change out of his suit pocket. "I happen to know they have coffee shops and bakeries in the Altstadt. This is quite a departure from your daily routine. Why did you go so far out of your way?"

He handed her the money, and he didn't pull his hand away when their fingers touched. "I would think that would be obvious." He raised his coffee cup to her before turning to leave. "See you later."

Obvious? Not really. Katja was stunned. Had Micah traipsed all the way across town just to see her? It didn't make sense, especially since they saw each other every single evening. She stared at his back as he left the store, worrying the ring in her lip.

"So, is that your boyfriend?" Renata's voice interrupted her thoughts.

She arched an eyebrow at her boss. "I'm not sure."

KISS ME GOOD

KATJA SNIFFED and moaned as she stirred awake the next morning. Her body was stiff and she ached all over. She could barely lift herself out of bed to use the bathroom. Her head was burning up. She splashed cold water on her face, then promptly vomited in the toilet.

She went back to her place on the sofa bed with a bucket and a cold cloth and passed out.

She stands on an older, wooden bridge that crosses a raging waterfall. The bridge is shifting and cracking. She has to get off or she will fall and surely die, but her legs won't move! She opens her mouth to scream, but nothing comes out.

Micah's there now. Beautiful, brave Micah. He sees she's in danger and he runs to save her. But no, the bridge is falling. If he reaches for her he'll fall, too. She shouts, "No!"

Katja's eyes sprung open as she called out.

"Shh," a voice said.

She collapsed to her bed and calmed her breathing, vaguely aware of someone helping her, holding her head up so she could sip water, wiping her brow. She was in and out. No more dreams. Just blackness.

Katja finally woke to the early morning light, but it came in from the wrong direction. She stirred feeling discombobulated. This wasn't her bed. These weren't her sheets.

Her eyes popped open.

This was Micah's room. His bed. Her eyes scanned the surface for another form, but she was there alone.

So, where was Micah?

She slipped out from beneath the sheets, waiting a moment for the dizziness to pass, then padded softly to the living room. He was sleeping on her spot on the sofa bed. She was relieved to find him, but confused.

Why had they switched places?

His eyes opened and focused on her. "Feeling better?"

"Yes. I guess so. What happened? Why are you sleeping there?"

Micah pushed himself up into a sitting position, the sheet falling to his waist, exposing his toned, bare chest. Katja glanced away.

"You came down with a serious flu. You were out for two days. The doctor came by and helped me move you. He said if you weren't doing better by today to take you to the hospital."

Two days?

Micah slipped a T-shirt over his head and tugged it down. "I'm relieved you're feeling better."

"Me, too," Katja said, though her legs felt shaky. She didn't smell great, either. "I'm going to have a shower."

She let the hot water pour on her head and scrubbed off the sweat and sickness. She didn't remember getting into Micah's bed. He must've carried her.

She dressed in jeans and a light blouse. They felt looser. She'd lost weight.

"Would you like coffee?" Micah said when she walked out. "Breakfast? Do you feel like eating?"

She combed her fingers through her damp hair. "Actually, I'm starving."

He closed the distance between them and stroked her face. "You scared me."

His words surprised her, and she didn't know what to say. He stepped away and smiled. "One coffee and breakfast platter coming up!"

She picked at the soft-boiled eggs and toast Micah presented, doing her best to prove she was on the mend. They chuckled over breakfast, gossiping about the other tenants in the building. Katja studied him as he ate. He'd changed since the "ceremony." His countenance was lighter. He seemed happier.

Was he happy?

"I dreamed about you this morning," she said.

He winked. "A make-out dream?"

"No!" She clasped a hand over her mouth to hide a smile birthed from embarrassment. She couldn't believe he'd said that. "It was actually a scary dream. You were in danger."

His expression grew serious. "How so?"

"You were trying to save me, and in doing so, you were about to lose your own life."

He didn't respond. The only noise in the room she could hear was the pounding of her heart. "Are you trying to save me, Micah?"

He considered her. "Do you need saving?"

She twisted her lips to the side, then said, "Maybe, but don't deflect."

"You think I'm helping you so I can atone for my guilt about losing Greta."

Katja leaned back and folded her arms over her chest. "The thought has crossed my mind."

Micah mimicked her, crossing his arms and leaning

back as well. "I'm not. And I'm not going to apologize for trying to save you, if or when you need saving."

Katja almost said she didn't need saving. But Micah had saved her the night he picked her up off the streets. And he did just take care of her when she was so sick she didn't even know she'd been sleeping in his bed.

Then Micah smiled. "Well, I think we're both safe enough for today. The sun is shining. Do you feel up for a walk along the river?"

Katja softened her posture. A walk would be nice.

She used the bathroom and brushed her teeth. Her hair was still a little damp, one of the hazards of having so much thick hair. She spent a few minutes with the blow dryer until her locks were thoroughly dry, then she pulled it all back into a high ponytail. She chose a light silk scarf to match her blouse and donned a summer sweater while waiting for Micah to take his turn in the bathroom.

He hung a hoodie over his shoulder then opened the door allowing Katja to leave first, and then he locked the door behind them. He followed her down the stairs. She held the rail still feeling a little weak.

"Are you okay?" Micah asked, noticing. "We don't have to go out if you're not up to it."

"I'm fine," she said. "I want to go."

Once outside, Micah surprised her by wrapping an arm around her waist, and she leaned in grateful that he was there to hold her up. She reached up to her shoulder and clasped his hand, squeezing gently, happy they were growing more comfortable with each other.

They found an empty bench and sat facing the sun. Micah kept his arm around Katja as if it were the most natural thing in the world. He studied her profile like she was a painting, and her heart skipped a beat. She melted under the gaze of his dark eyes. He leaned over to kiss her forehead and paused. Katja tilted her chin up. Micah was looking at her lips. She parted them.

"I think it's time you kissed me," she said. "Kissed me good."

Micah grinned crookedly. "I think you're right."

He cupped her face, and she ran her fingers through his dark curls. His lips landed on hers, taking her breath away. This was it. They were *together*.

Finally, Katja thought.

They kissed slowly, and Katja lingered on every moment. She wanted to memorize the taste of his lips, the feel of them on hers, soft and sensuous. The way he trailed kisses along her jaw, to the base of her neck and back again. She closed her eyes and felt light as a feather, like she was floating away, without a single care. Safe and adored. She couldn't remember being happier than she was in this moment, kissing Micah on a park bench in the sun.

PLAY FOR ME

THEY WALKED LANGUIDLY over the blackened, stone bridge to the old town in search of a place to eat lunch. The sky was cerulean blue, and the rippling water of the Elbe sparkled in the sun. Katja felt like the world was crisp, distinctive and spectacularly beautiful. They held hands over the table at an outdoor restaurant and ordered braised chicken salads with lemon dressing and sour dough buns. The flavors were exquisite and her taste buds delighted in the meal. She couldn't believe how this day had become so amazing, and her gaze washed over Micah's face as they ate and conversed.

Every subject was so much more tantalizing: music, books, movies, current events, technology, travel dreams.

Afterward, they visited the art museum, window shopped at the gift shops and watched actors in front of the arches who dressed like statues and stood stiff and unblinking. They stopped at the neighborhood grocery store to pick up supplies for the meal they planned to make together later that evening, like a real couple.

Katja almost burst at the seams with happiness. This was the perfect day. Maybe the best day of her whole life.

The groceries were barely put away before they ended up making out on the sofa. They moaned and giggled, and

Katja was ready to give everything away to Micah. She'd never felt this strongly about anyone before, and the thought occurred to her that she was falling in love.

Micah gently pushed her back, taking a deep breath.

"I think we should slow things down a little." He stroked her cheek with his finger and rested his forehead against hers. "The best things in life are savored, experienced gradually over time."

Katja smiled. Micah was right. Even though it was so tempting to eat a whole jar of candy in one sitting, no one was happy with how they felt afterward.

Micah gestured to her guitar. "Play for me."

It was a simple request, but one that made Katja abnormally nervous. Micah had heard her play before, but always in a group setting at one of her gigs. She rarely practiced or wrote songs when he was home, not since her feelings for him had started to grow. It just felt… too vulnerable.

"I don't know," she responded. "Why don't you turn the stereo on instead?"

"Katja, please." He tilted his head, and grinned playfully. "Sing for me."

Katja hesitated, then removed her guitar from its case. She laid it across her lap and pressed her fingers to the strings, adjusting the tuning pegs to bring them in tune. Playing and singing was such a normal creative expression for her, but for some reason, today, alone with Micah, she felt like she was about to bare her soul.

"What do you want to hear?"

"Have you written anything new?"

She nodded and her tongue reached for the ring in her lip. Was she ready to play it for Micah? He'd know the lyrics were about them. She strummed the first chord and dove in.

It's all in how you look at it,
she said
As if there were a hundred ways to walk a high wire
Go on and try to let it go
Close your eyes and
Let your heart rule your head sometimes
Some folks dig for gold
and only scratch the surface
You saw something more
and it's making you nervous

Maybe he'd think it was about something else, and not about her deepening emotions about the man who stared so intently at every move she made with her fingers and every word that formed on her lips.

She stopped suddenly, and glanced away. "That's all I have for now."

"Katja, you are so talented, so artistic." Micah said. His eyebrows jumped. "It's very tantalizing."

She giggled and plucked out a random lick on the strings.

"When did you know you wanted to be a musician?" He stroked her arm. "Tell me how it happened."

"I can't remember a day when I didn't love music," she responded. "When I was young, before my father left, my mother always had music playing on the radio in our kitchen. Even as a baby I banged out rhythms on the table when I was supposed to be eating my Nutella toast.

"Dad actually boasted about me to his friends, and one day he came home with a beat up guitar. I don't know where he got it, flea market, likely. I guess I have my father to thank for something. My hands were too small, and I couldn't do anything but mess around for a while, but I eventually grew into it. I never got any lessons. I figured out the basic chords and just taught myself by playing my favorite songs. There are a lot of guitar lessons posted on YouTube. Henni's family had a computer, and I spent hours every Sunday afternoon practicing at her place, pretty much force feeding myself on those. That and the songwriting videos."

Katja paused to run a finger along the curves of her guitar. "I worked hard the summer I was sixteen, cooking *bratwurst* sausages at my neighbor's stand in the park. I was too shy to sing in front of anyone at first, just played to myself in the privacy of my bedroom. I spent the summer evenings with Henni, watching the street musicians on *Unter den Linden* and how random strangers filled up their instrument cases with coins. I realized it was a way for me to make some money without standing on my feet all day in the summer heat.

"The first time I did it was the result of a dare." She glanced over her shoulder at the memory. "Henni and I were playing Truth or Dare with a bunch of the complex kids. She knew about my secret obsession and dared me to busk or to kiss chubby Bernhart Moser on the lips."

Micah laughed, and Katja hurried to conclude her story. "I chose busking, of course. She made me do it right that instant. I ran inside to get my guitar, and everyone followed me to the nearest pedestrians-only shopping street. I was scared to death but more afraid of kissing Bernhart. I closed my eyes and played and unbelievably, people tossed coins into my case. My friends cheered me on, and after that I was hooked. The next thing I knew I was trying out at all the open mic spots I could find. I met someone who helped me record in their home studio, and then I had CDs. It just kind of happened."

"Do you miss Berlin?"

"The city? Sure."

"Not your family?"

Katja closed her eyes, knowing where this conversation was headed. Micah continued before she could answer.

"I have a business meeting coming up there next Saturday. I can go with my colleagues, Anna and Thomas, but…" He looked at her expectantly. "If you wanted to go, we could drive together. My meeting's over at 1:00. We could swing by your home for an hour or so and be home that evening."

Katja's heart jumped at the thought of going away with Micah, even if it was only a two hour drive north of Dresden, but then it plummeted again at the idea of going "home."

"I don't know."

"Katja." His gaze softened, and he leaned closer. "It's very difficult to have someone you care about go missing. Have you called your sister yet?"

"Not yet, but I will."

"And you'll go with me to Berlin?"

Katja sighed. "Can I get back to you on that one?"

Micah squeezed her knee. "Sure. Now sing me another song."

I'M NOT THAT PERSON ANYMORE

THAT NIGHT MICAH entered the living room with clean sheets in his hands. "I've already changed the ones on my bed. Go ahead. I want you to sleep there."

Katja squinted. "Alone?"

Micah smirked. "For now."

He was right, she supposed. It had taken them three months to get to their first kissing session, she shouldn't expect him to sleep with her the first night they got together. Though she wouldn't argue with him if he tried.

"I can sleep here," she said, pointing to the sofa. "I don't want to kick you out of your bed."

Micah dropped the sheets and took her hand. "I want you in my bed. Believe me, it makes me very happy to know you're there."

"But, why don't you come, too?"

Micah leaned back and ducked down. "Call me old-fashioned but I won't sleep with a girl unless I'm committing my whole life. I don't want a woman just for her body."

"Did you sleep with Greta?"

Oh, God. Why did she just say that?

Micah's expression turned cold. He let her go. "I'm not the person I used to be. I thought you knew that."

130

He turned away, and she quickly reached for his hand. "Micah, I'm sorry. I don't know why I said that."

His eyes grew soft, and he pulled her close again, resting his chin on her head. "It's okay. Our situation is unusual."

No kidding.

He tugged her to the sofa and pulled her on his lap. "Let me try to explain. After Greta disappeared, I did a lot of soul-searching. I took a long, hard look at myself, the kind of person I was, and I didn't like what I saw. I quit drinking and doing drugs. Girls would come on to me, many of Greta's friends, in fact. Why, I don't know. Maybe to comfort me, but probably to conquer something that had belonged to a rival, but I wasn't even tempted."

He shrugged. "I guess you could say I experienced a type of spiritual awakening."

Katja wasn't sure what to think about that. She believed in God, but she certainly didn't believe he cared about her that much, not after what she'd been through.

He continued, "Somewhere along the line I'd heard this concept of soul ties."

"Soul ties?" Katja asked, feeling more confused than ever.

"Yeah. People aren't just flesh and blood. They're soul and spirit, too. When two people join physically, they also join spiritually, creating a soul-tie with each other. The two become one."

Katja couldn't resist scoffing. "That's crazy."

Micah's expression stayed stoic. "I don't think it is. In fact, it makes perfect sense to me. The more people you sleep with, the more soul ties you make. It explains why so many people are ridiculously screwed up, bringing a boat-load of baggage into each new relationship. Think about it."

Katja was thinking about it, and she didn't buy it.

"What if I don't believe in it?"

"Then I hope you will be patient with me. Because I do."

Katja had no choice but to honor his beliefs. She agreed to go easy on him, though she wouldn't stop him from doing anything if he tried. He had to exercise his own willpower.

It was a peculiar kiss goodnight. Katja had changed into her nightshirt, and Micah wore his T-shirt and pajama pants. They were like two magnets with large, invisible hands trying to keep them apart, but their pull was so strong they kept snapping back together. They performed this awkward dance down the hall until they came to Micah's room. She tugged on his shirt, but the doorway was like a force field Micah steadfastly refused to penetrate. He broke free of her grasp, leaving them both gasping like dying goldfish. He ran a hand through his hair and let out a loud raspy breath.

"Goodnight, Katja!" He turned and practically ran down the hall until he disappeared.

Katja held a hand to her chest. She didn't know how they were going to survive this night after night. It would take her a long time to calm down. She lay down and rolled over to face the other side of the bed.

Her eyes adjusted to the dimly lit room and landed on a sheet of paper attached to the wall. She recognized the size. It came from her sketch pad. She reached for the reading lamp and turned it on. She squinted and took in a short breath. It was her Sun & Moon drawing.

Now that she knew what had been in the locked room, she understood why Micah had taken it down. That room represented Greta. The drawing represented her.

He'd moved it to his room. Somehow it felt right. It made her glad.

She felt her face pull into a relaxed smile, and eventually she fell asleep.

Micah left early the next morning for work, before Katja was out of bed. This was normal, but she decided to wake earlier in the future so she could share breakfast with him and kiss him goodbye.

She worked the nine-to-three shift at the coffee shop, and couldn't have removed the smile from her face or the spring in her step to save her life.

Renata laughed. "My guess is that handsome, young man *is* your boyfriend now."

Katja smiled like a fool. "He is, Renata, and I'm so happy. He's kind, and thoughtful and a gentleman. And he's hot!"

Renata's eyes sparkled, enjoying the bliss. "You've fallen hard, my young friend."

Katja wiped the counter with a damp cloth, trying to regain her composure, but the grin just wouldn't leave her face. "I know. I'm in deep trouble."

Renata laughed louder.

"What about you?" Katja ventured. Renata had told her about her failed marriage, but she'd been single for ten years.

Renata shot her a puzzled look. "What about me?"

"Isn't it time you found love again?"

Renata snorted. "Once is enough for me, thank you."

"But what if there was someone else? Wouldn't you like to be in love again?"

"Oh, goodness. I'm too old for that, I think."

"I don't think so." In fact, Katja had the perfect guy in mind. If only she could think of a way to introduce Renata to Maurice. "Just don't rule it out. Life's too short."

Renata laughed again and waved her away. "In love for one day, and now you're the expert."

After work, Katja bought the groceries she and Micah needed for dinner. She put the food away, changed into clean clothes and freshened her makeup. Then she waited on the steps of the apartment building for Micah to arrive back from work. A warm flush of joy spread through her body when she spotted him walking toward her, and her face broke out into a huge smile. He sat beside her, and wove his fingers through hers before leaning in for a long, delicious kiss.

It was a routine that repeated day after day. She'd wait for him on the building steps, and he'd sit with her and kiss her good on the lips until their famished state drove them inside. They'd have dinner and then make out on the sofa until they were panting and charged with so much chemistry and electricity that Katja thought they'd set the place on fire. She was certain Micah would break his personal vow and carry her to his room, but every night he stopped them before they went too far.

She seriously wondered if she was going to have to wait for him to propose. Maybe she should move out (for real!), just for the sake of their sanity. Staying here with Micah like this was torture.

She almost brought up the idea, but the thought of leaving Micah's flat was too painful. She'd just have to learn to deal.

FINALLY, ANOTHER GIG

KATJA HAD APPLIED to participate in the folk music festival in Dresden a year ago. She knew they didn't have a way of contacting her, so she used her new phone to call them, hoping to use the excuse that she wanted to update her contact info to remind them that she existed and to please, pretty please, let her play.

She kept the begging to her imagination, but giving them her new phone number was a smart move. They called a week later. She was in.

Katja excitedly told Micah about it when he got home from work. "Can you come?" she asked him.

"I wouldn't miss it," he said. "In fact, I'm going to invite my work colleagues."

"Are they musicians?" Katja asked.

"You don't have to be a musician to love music."

Katja realized she hadn't even met any of Micah's friends. He was new to Dresden, like she was, so he probably didn't know a lot of people. And, until recently, he wasn't exactly outgoing. She smiled to herself, knowing that she played a big part in his coming out of his shell. She liked this new Micah. Really, *really* liked him.

Katja spent a few days stewing over what she should wear on stage. She didn't have a large wardrobe and virtually no stage clothes, whatever that meant. A trip to the second hand store solved her problems. She found a great ankle-length, flouncy skirt and a white, cotton peasant blouse. She also picked up a head band and silver jewelry. With her leather strap sandals, she'd look the part of a seventies festival hippy, which, with her long, wavy hair, suited her and added to her artist brand.

Micah grinned and pulled her into a frisky embrace when he saw her. "You're my very own Janis Joplin."

The festival wasn't within walking distance, so Micah drove them there, though they still had to park a good ways away. Micah offered to carry her guitar.

"Man, this thing's heavy!" he said, eyeing her. He reached for her biceps and squeezed, causing her to giggle and pull away.

"That tickles!" she said.

Micah smiled mischievously. "I'll keep that in mind."

When they arrived, they went through the special entrance just for artists and festival crew. Katja introduced herself and Micah to the organizer. He gave her an artist pass, and a plus-one pass for Micah, then filled her in on her time slot, and when she should be ready and waiting back stage.

"This is kind of cool," Micah said. "I feel like a groupie."

Katja threaded her arm through his. "You're *my* groupie."

"That works for me," he said. "From now on, you can introduce me as your personal groupie."

They entered the grounds with the rest of the festival goers and listened for a while to the act playing on stage. It was a reggae band, and Katja grooved to the beat. Micah tugged on her arm and spoke into her ear. "Anna and Thomas are here."

In the throng of people, she couldn't tell who he was pointing at. She followed him until they stopped in front of a guy and girl in their mid-twenties. For some reason Katja imagined Micah's colleagues to be older and frumpier and boring.

Thomas wore a tight shirt tucked into very slim pants. He shook Katja's hand politely but his eyes didn't register any interest. She got the impression he wasn't into girls like her. Or girls at all, for that matter.

Anna was young and stylish and *not* frumpy. She wore a very short summer dress with fashionable wedge-heeled sandals, and her auburn hair was pulled up in a high pony-tail with a backcombed and heavily hair-sprayed bump on top.

She looked like British royalty out to mingle with the common folk. Katja suddenly felt like the frumpy one and second-guessed her choice of wardrobe. What was she thinking?

"Micah and I graduated from university in Hamburg together," Anna said as she shook Katja's hand. "Small world that we'd end up working at the same financial insti-tution." She smiled at Micah. "It's so nice to have someone around everyday who enjoys talking about the markets."

Micah *enjoys* talking about the *markets*?

Now, not only did she feel dressed like a peasant, she also felt uneducated. How long before Micah bored of their casual, lower-classed conversation? Micah came from wealth and academia. That was his world. She was from a different planet entirely.

Suddenly her chest grew heavy like her ribs were caving in. No one else seemed aware of how the earth had just shifted. She refocused on the conversation between Micah and Anna, something about a business meeting in Berlin.

Right. That was this Saturday.

Anna laughed and patted Micah on the arm.

"Micah and I are going together," Katja heard herself say. "I have family there."

Anna's face went blank. Micah glanced at Katja with interest. "So you've decided? For sure?"

Katja nodded adamantly. There was no way she was shipping Micah off to spend the day alone with Market-Happy Anna. "Yeah, I'm sure."

She dragged Micah away with the guise of having to find something to drink. They bought bottled water and Katja took a long swig.

"Is everything all right?" Micah asked.

She couldn't admit to having a jealous bout. "I'm just nervous. I should probably get backstage soon."

"Okay. I'm going to find a spot up front and center. If you get too nervous, just look at me."

Katja smiled and gave him a hug. She was grateful for his offer, but *he* was the one who was making her nervous.

She went backstage as instructed, tuned her guitar and double-checked her strap. She hummed to warm up her voice.

She heard the emcee introduce her. "I'm pleased to introduce one of Dresden's own, Katja Stoltz!"

The crowd responded with polite applause. She wasn't a headliner and only had a three song slot, but she was there to show everyone what she was made of and get her name out there. Eventually, she'd be invited to bigger stages and given longer slots and better pay. At least that was the plan.

"Hi everyone," she began. "Thank you for having me."

Katja began with the two original songs she knew well, *Think Back* and *Sun & Moon*. The first spoke to her about why it was a good idea for her to go home, and not only so she could keep Anna away from Micah. The second song reminded her of how far she and Micah had come. In life and in their relationship.

She watched him like he'd asked her to. He smiled like the proud boyfriend he was and clapped louder than anyone between songs.

"Thank you," she said at the end. "The last song I'm going to perform for you is brand new. I hope you like it."

She began the song she had started for Micah a few nights ago. Their eyes connected and her stomach swirled with nerves. She had to pull her gaze away and focus if she wanted to get through this song successfully. She closed her eyes.

It's all in how you look at it,
she said
As if there were a hundred ways to walk a high wire
Go on and try to let it go
Close your eyes and
Let your heart rule your head sometimes
Some folks dig for gold and only scratch the surface
You saw something more and it's making you nervous
How deep can you feel?
Could you really let this get to you?
How far can this all go?
Could you really change your point of view?
Let the best of you become undone
Look past your logic and all that other noise
You're always looking
For the answers,
she said
But sometimes it's all about the questioning
You never seem to let it show

But that's all right
Cause I know your heart is a deep, deep well
Some folks dig for gold
And only scratch the surface
Sometimes a mystery can have another purpose

The crowd applauded boisterously and enthusiastically just like she'd hoped. The stage manager gave her a high five.

"You killed it, girl!"

Micah was waiting for her when she came off the stage.

"That's a pretty intense song," he said, standing inches away, face to face. "Was it about you or about me?"

"Both, I think."

He cupped her cheeks with his hands. "I think I have a celebrity crush. You were amazing."

Katja's heart danced. Micah's praise meant the world to her. "Thank you."

He kissed her before she could say anything more, and she didn't complain.

THINK BACK TO WHEN YOU WERE A CHILD

TRAFFIC MOVED BRISKLY ALONG the autobahn as they traveled north in the direction of Berlin. It was early in the morning, the sky an ethereal mix of cobalt blue and burnt umber. Katja's gaze moved from the painted canvas of the skyline to Micah's profile. His left hand rested on the Audi's steering wheel while his right hand wrapped lazily around the stick shift. He focused on expertly maneuvering into the fast lane, confirming to Katja that they'd make it there in good time.

The prospect of seeing her family again caused her stomach to twirl, and she worked to push those thoughts aside. Instead, she inwardly sketched the lines of Micah's face on an imaginary canvas. He was the perfect subject, and she itched to get what she envisioned in her head on paper.

His eyes cut to hers. "You're staring at me."

"An astute observation."

"It's not fair. Maybe you should drive next time, so I can stare at you."

Katja smiled. "No chance."

Not long afterward, Micah pulled into a rest stop. Katja dug through her purse looking for the fifty cents she needed to use the facilities. Then she remembered. She'd thrown all her tip money into the fruit bowl yesterday.

Micah grinned and removed a fist from his front pocket producing a handful of coins. "Allow me."

Katja sheepishly plucked out the needed coinage and dropped them into the slot that moved the gate allowing her entrance. After using the toilet, she washed her hands in the sink and stared at her reflection in the mirror. She hadn't seen her family in nearly six months. Had she changed much? Yes, she had. Her hair was a few inches longer, but that wasn't the marked difference. No, it was her face. It was leaner, her cheekbones sharper, her eyes wider, less naive.

She was older and wiser, but still frightened. The younger version of herself was curled up inside, shackled with insecurities and vulnerabilities resulting from unpredictable, shifting boundaries. Home wasn't a place to gain support and good advice. She could never find her footing there. It was like walking on the rain-soaked deck of a swaying boat in a storm.

She closed her eyes and let out a long breath. Why had she let Micah talk her into this?

No, he hadn't. It was her decision. She was stronger now. She could do this.

She dried her hands and took a few moments to reapply her mascara and lip gloss. When she re-entered the store, Micah had just finished purchasing a package of gummy candies.

"Want some?"

It was pretty early for candy, but Katja felt like she'd been up for half a day already. She opened her palm and he shook the bag until several fell in. "Thanks," she said, tossing one into her mouth.

They hit rush hour traffic when they entered the outskirts of the city.

"It's a good thing we left early," Micah said, tapping his fingers on the wheel.

The plan was to park the car in underground parking in the middle of Berlin near where Micah's meeting was taking place. He'd suggested that she go visit her family while he was there, but she didn't want to go alone. In the end, he agreed that she could wander the city until his meeting ended and they could go to see her family together.

Micah removed his briefcase and suit jacket from the back seat, slipping the latter item on. His white shirt fell untucked over jeans, and he nailed the preppy, urban, young business man look.

"Are you sure you'll be okay?" he asked again.

"Yes. This is my town." She smiled reassuringly. "I'm looking forward to meandering the streets again."

"Make sure you eat something," he said. "They'll be feeding us, so I'll be fine." He pulled fifty euro from his pocket and slipped it into her hand.

"I have a job, you know," she said, staring at the bill. She stretched her arm to give it back.

"I know. I'd just feel better if you took it. Do it for me."

She shrugged and slipped the money in her pocket. She wouldn't spend it. It would find its way into the fruit bowl later that night. But it did make her feel good that Micah desired to take care of her.

Katja kissed Micah longingly, wanting it to be memorable enough to last through whatever close encounters he might have with Anna. She ran her tongue along his lips, nibbling the bottom one as she pulled away. By the smile and glint she saw in his eye, she thought she succeeded.

"See you in four hours," he said, walking backward to the glass doors of the banking institution.

Katja felt bereft for a moment, but then shifted her backpack and straightened her stance. She took in her surroundings and started walking. She was on the eastern side of Brandenburg Gate. It was a huge stone monument comprised of six deep pillars creating five archways and was topped with a greening bronze statue of four racing horses pulling a chariot with a lone rider. The gate had signified communistic rule for forty years and now freedom that came with the subsequent democracy. Crowds milled about, tourists mostly, taking pictures and lining up to hop on the tour buses.

She hadn't been born yet when the wall came down, but change came slowly, and growing up in eastern Berlin was very much an Eastern-Bloc experience for her. She lived in a concrete block apartment in the lower-income part of the city that had been built during the GDR times. It was the same one her family still resided in, with only two bedrooms, a small kitchen and living area. The grounds were left in their natural state, with landscaping reserved for parks, tourist destinations and higher-income dwellings.

She'd learned a lot about the value of freedom. Her mother used to tell her there was nothing more important than that. Her grandparents had all passed away before the wall fell, and had never experienced what it was like to pass through the Brandenburg Gate to the western side since it had been barricaded by the Berlin Wall.

Katja was fortunate to be born in a time when physical freedom had been granted to Europeans, but that didn't mean she was completely free. There were bondages known to the human psyche that didn't involve physical chains or armed border patrols.

She walked through the massive columns to the west side until she was in the Tiergarten, a green space that claimed several city blocks, and settled on an unoccupied park bench. She removed her notepads from her pack. Was she in the mood to write or draw?

Neither was calling to her at the moment. She gazed ahead blankly as a childhood memory crystallized. Her father and mother had brought her here once, when she was three or four years old. There was a fair of some kind set up in the park, and her parents had taken her on a ride. It was a bland one, where they sat in a small chair and spun in lazy circles. But she remembered being thrilled, her mother on one side and her father on the other, both of them squishing her in the middle. She laughed out loud, not truly understanding the source of her joy. She'd thought it was the ride. She now knew it was because they were together, a family.

Melancholy dripped on her like dew. A sadness for what could've been. Grief for what was lost when her father left them.

She'd never known why. Against her mother's wishes he'd taken a job fishing in the northern sea. They hadn't seen him since. Why hadn't he tried to contact her? Why did he stop loving her?

Katja put her notebooks into her bag. She headed back to the eastern side where most of the shopping was. She walked up and down *Unter Den Linden*, browsing the gift shops and bookstores. She stopped at a donair place and bought a gyros sandwich for two euro. She wondered mildly what exactly Micah thought she would eat for lunch that she'd need fifty euro. Steak and lobster?

A quick check of the time on her phone told her she had only twenty-five minutes left to wait. The time had gone by quickly. She slowly worked her way back to the bank to meet up with Micah.

He was huddled on the front steps with Thomas and Anna when she arrived. Katja plastered on a smile and shimmied up behind him.

"Oh, hi," he said, wrapping an arm around her shoulders for a quick hug. He wasn't shy to show his affection in front of his friends, and Katja shook off her feelings of inadequacy. Micah *liked* her. Micah was into *her*.

She even flashed a genuine smile Anna's way. Anna blinked and then returned it. Katja tugged on Micah's hand. "Time to go?"

They said goodbye and walked around the corner to the car. "How was your meeting?" Katja asked.

"Oh, you know. Boring."

"Boring? I thought you loved all that markets and money talk."

He shrugged. "It's interesting enough, but it's just a job."

Micah started the car and stopped to stare at her before driving out. "You're ready for this?"

No. "As ready as I'll ever be."

Katja gave Micah directions to the dense, multi-family residence where her family lived. She completely regretted bringing Micah when they pulled to a stop in front of the colorless building. Weeds grew out of the sidewalk cracks and took over whatever yard existed between the building and the road. There'd been some effort to paint the exterior over the years, but wind and rain had worn it away in spots, and it peeled away from the cracking plaster. Laundry hung on clothes lines, and several people leaned out open windows smoking cigarettes and blatantly stared at them. The Audi didn't belong in this neighborhood. Neither did Micah Sturm.

"It's not too late to turn around," Katja whimpered.

Micah squeezed her hand. "We're here now. You can do it."

She inhaled deeply and opened the door. It felt so strange to be back, even though she'd walked down this path to the front door of her building a million times. She hesitated at the door, before inserting her key.

She led Micah up the dimly lit stairwell to the second floor. The air inside was a stale mix of cigarette smoke and the odor of the six families who shared the floor: dirty laundry and last night's dinner.

She paused in the hallway outside of their door. "This is it."

"Are you going to knock?" he asked.

"I guess so. I mean, I've never knocked before, but I'd never been away so long before either."

"Then knock."

"They might not be home."

"You won't find out if you don't knock."

She puffed, hating that he was so pragmatic, and tapped on the door. The rumble of the neighbor's TV bled through into the hall from the opposite side, so Katja couldn't hear if there was movement in her flat.

"I don't think anyone's here," she said just moments before the door inched open. A set of wide, blue eyes stared at her. "Katja?"

"Hi, Sibylle."

Her younger sister opened the door, and Katja spread her arms, inviting her in for an embrace. Sibylle hesitated, then stepped forward, but her thin arms didn't reciprocate.

"How are you?"

Sibylle's mouth remained pulled down in a frown. "Okay."

"You've grown." Her sister was almost twelve and had

started filling out. Katja smiled to hide her concern. Sibylle was at the age she had been when Horst started acting inappropriately with her.

"Who's that?" Sibylle asked.

Katja turned to Micah, whose eyes had moved from her sister to the space beyond. The place was filthy. Dirty dishes filled the limited counter space, and the living area was unkempt with abandoned food containers and dirty clothes lying about. Again Katja wished she'd come alone.

"This is my friend Micah."

"Hello," Micah said gently.

Sibylle glanced away shyly. "Hi."

Katja looked beyond her sister for signs that anyone else was there with her. "Is Mama home?"

"She's in her room."

Katja swallowed but kept her voice even. "What about your dad?"

Sibylle shrugged. "I don't know where he is. I'll get Mama."

A burning sensation built up behind Katja's eyes. She hated seeing her sister so despondent. Like a miniature version of her mother. She smiled weakly over her shoulder at Micah. He gave her a slight nod.

An impossibly thin woman with greasy hair and ragged clothes padded into the room. "Katja?" she said faintly. "Is that you?"

Katja nodded. "Yes, Mama."

The woman covered her mouth with a bony hand, and her shoulders began to shake. "You look good," she managed to say through a soft sob. "I was so worried."

"Oh, Mama." Katja almost ran to her mother and pulled her into a hug. "I'm fine. I'm doing great. I met someone wonderful." She waved Micah over. "This is my friend Micah. Micah, my mother, Frau Bergmann."

Katja's mother wiped her eyes, then held out her hand. "Thank you for taking care of my daughter."

"It's been my pleasure."

"And please, call me Gisela."

"Sibylle," Gisela said, "Put a pot on for tea."

Katja's sister ran water into the pot and turned on the old stove. Gisela made an effort to clean a space at the table. "I'm sorry it's so messy. If I knew you were coming…"

"It's fine, Mama."

Katja and Micah sat awkwardly at the table while her sister and mother made tea and served it to them in old but clean teacups.

"We're out of milk and sugar," Gisela said.

"Black is fine," Micah said, thanking her.

Gisela lowered herself into the chair adjacent to Katja's. "Tell us all about your adventures."

Katja's eyes cut to Micah, and he encouraged her with a tip of his chin. She told them about her gigs, and her job at the coffee shop. "It's not super exciting, but it's good."

Gisela motioned to Micah. "How did you meet this fine young man?"

The way they met will forever be a point of embarrassment. Katja wondered if other couples had to lie about their first encounters. Micah came to her rescue. "We met outside a restaurant in Dresden. I thought she was someone else at first, but I'm glad for the mistake now; otherwise, we wouldn't have had a reason to talk."

It was a cleaned-up version, but it wasn't untrue.

"Lovely," her mother said.

Sibylle disappeared into the living area, where she turned on the TV. Katja sipped her tea, working up the courage to ask her mother the question that had forever been burning on her heart. "Mama, I was wondering... Why did Dad leave?"

"He'll be back soon. He's just dating Jack Daniels." It was meant to be a joke, but she didn't smile.

"No," Katja clarified. "I mean *my* father. Why did he leave us?"

"Oh." Gisela drew back and wrung her hands in her lap. Katja thought for a moment that she wouldn't answer, but then she mumbled. "I know I told you he left us. It was because I was angry. He worked at a mill near here, and even though it didn't pay well, I was happy enough with that. Between the two of us, we got by. But then he heard about the fishing job with big promises of large wages. I begged him not to quit his job and leave us, but he wouldn't listen. He promised to send me money— lots of money, he said—but instead, I never heard from him for months. On my wage alone, it wasn't enough to take care of us."

Gisela wiped her eyes. "A year later, I got a telegram saying he fell off the boat. I never saw one dime of any money he supposedly made."

Katja felt tears burn at the back of her eyes. "He fell off the boat? You mean he *died*?"

Gisela's eyes drooped. "I should've told you, I know. But I thought that thinking he was gone would be easier for you than knowing he was dead."

Katja sat back stunned. She supposed that deep down she knew something terrible had happened to her father. She'd believed he'd loved her and wouldn't have stayed away so long if he were alive and of sound mind somewhere.

But hearing the truth so starkly like that pierced her heart. Sorrow weighed heavily for the things both she and her mother had lost by her father's poor decision.

Oh, Papa. At least when she thought he was alive, there was hope they might meet up again. Now that hope was shattered and her heart along with it. She let her hair fall in front of her face to hide the grief that pinched so deeply. But knowing that her father hadn't abandoned them, that he *meant* to do them well, brought some relief. Maybe now she could forgive him for not being there for her, for forcing her mother to depend on Horst.

Katja reached up under her sheath of hair to press back the tears. She felt the warmth of Micah's palm on her leg under the table. Gisela reached across the table for her hand. "I'm sorry."

Katja didn't know how to respond to her mother. It wasn't okay that she'd lied to her all these years. But, her mother wasn't strong, and she had done what she thought was best at the time.

Katja knew she needed to mourn this new loss, but now wasn't the right time. She breathed deeply and pushed her hair off her face. She mustered a soft, "It's okay." Then she dug her phone out of her bag, surreptitiously checked the time under the table and glanced at Micah. She wanted to leave.

"I have a phone now," she said to her mother. She took a pen and paper out of her purse and jotted down her number. "If you or Sibylle need anything, just call."

Katja sipped the last of her tea. Micah had been right about her coming back to check in. Her mother and sister didn't look great, but they were okay. And the fact that she had calmed her mother's worries made the effort worthwhile.

She was about to tell her mother they were leaving when the door opened and a low baritone voice she knew well slurred, "What the…?"

Horst stumbled into the room, and everyone automatically stiffened. Katja stood and Micah followed her lead.

"We were just leaving," she said.

Horst narrowed his puffy, bloodshot eyes. "Katja? Is that you?"

He lumbered his heavy form toward her and Katja's eyes widened with disbelief. He was actually going to try to embrace her? She stepped back, with palms up.

Horst's face twisted with offense. "What? You ungrateful sow! After everything I did for you, you can't even give your father a hug?"

"You're not my father," Katja said stiffly. "Never was, never will be."

He moved to grab her—Katja wasn't sure what he planned to do—but Micah stepped in between them. "Calm down," he said. He stood tall with straight shoulders and a stern glare. His fists curled near his abdomen.

"Or what?" Horst said incredulously. "You come into my home and think you're some big hot shot?"

Horst took a lazy swing, and Micah swiftly and expertly twisted his arm behind his back. Horst cried out in pain. Micah spoke clearly in his ear. "I'm leaving now with Katja. You make one wrong move and you're on the floor, do you understand?" He wrenched Horst's arm again, causing another yelp.

"And if you even think about touching your daughter in an inappropriate way or hurting your wife, I will send you a legion of trouble. You'll be locked up so long you'll never again see the light of day. Do you *understand?*"

"Yes, yes," Horst huffed.

Micah pushed him to the sofa where he collapsed. Katja quickly hugged her mother and sister, and whispered urgently into Sibylle's ear. "Mama has my phone number. Call me if you need me, okay?"

Sibylle's lips trembled but she nodded.

Katja hated leaving her mother and Sibylle behind, aware of how ironic it was considering she hadn't wanted to come to see them in the first place.

Besides fear and regret, her heart burned with another strong emotion: anger. And oddly it wasn't directed at Horst. She was mad at Micah.

THE FIGHT

Tension filled the Audi like foam peanut packaging in a parcel marked "fragile." Micah's white knuckles wrapped tightly around the steering wheel, his jaw clenched, and his eyes narrowed and trained on the road ahead. Katja stared out the passenger window, her arms folded over her chest and a thick lump forming in her throat.

"Are you okay?" Micah finally asked.

Katja bit her lip and shook her head once. No, she wasn't okay.

"I think things went well, though, hey? Until that jerk showed up."

"You shouldn't have done that."

Micah's eyes cut to Katja's stiff form. "Done what? Take down a bully?"

She turned sharply. "You don't get it, do you? You just made things infinitely worse."

"What? How?"

"You humiliated him in front of his wife and daughter. He's only going to get meaner now, to reinstate his status of patriarch."

Micah shook his head. "No. He understands that I'd bring the law down on his head if he did anything."

"The law doesn't care about people like my family."

Katja pinched back tears. "Women get beaten in their own homes all the time in my world. Girls get raped, and nothing ever happens to stop it. It's not like in your world where money talks and you can manipulate those less powerful than you with a simple threat."

Your world. My world. Katja held in a sob. Micah didn't get it. He didn't get *her*.

Silence filled the space, and an invisible force pushed them further apart. Katja lowered her window, suddenly needing fresh air. The world blurred by as the Audi picked up speed. Katja glanced at the speedometer: a hundred and eighty kilometers an hour.

"Look," Micah said through tight lips. "I'm sorry if I overstepped. Your step-dad was being a belligerent imbecile. I didn't have a chance to think it through." He reached for her arm and tugged until he found her hand, then threaded his fingers through hers.

"Your mother and sister were sweet. I'm glad I met them."

Katja's gaze moved from their joined hands to his face. Could he really mean that? Did he not see the squalor they lived in? That *she'd* grown up in? Her mother couldn't be more different than his fashion-conscious, high-powered mother.

He came from a world of privilege and entitlement, she from poverty and neglect. He might not think it mattered now, but it would. One day it would, and then what would she do? When the day came that Micah rejected her, what would she *do*?

A picture of her falling off the Augustus Bridge into the River Elbe flashed through her mind. The longer she stayed with Micah, the deeper the pain his parting would cause. Micah's grip remained, but she let her fingers go limp.

"This isn't going to work."

Micah signaled and pulled sharply off the road. His dark eyes flashed with anger as he stared at her. "You're not going to do this now."

She turned away, pinching her eyes tight. She wouldn't cry. Not here. Later, but not yet. Her lips tightened as they trembled. "You know I'm right."

He touched her shoulder. "Katja, look at me."

She didn't want to. She wanted to get back, pack her things and leave.

"Katja?"

She swallowed and looked at him. The look of longing in his eyes almost killed her resolve, but she breathed in deeply and stared back with determination. "You know I'm right," she repeated.

"I know no such thing."

"You might not want to see it now, but one day you will."

"One of us makes the other one feel small and cold," he quoted.

"Like the sun and the moon," she whispered back.

"I thought I was the moon," he said.

"No. It's always been me."

Micah sighed, then turned the Audi on and merged back onto the autobahn. The ride back to Dresden was quiet, the air between them, thick.

This was it, Katja thought. The end of their romance. She should've known better. She should've guarded her heart. Micah Sturm was too good for her. She'd never end up with someone like him. Never.

They entered Dresden and drove over the narrow, bumpy cobblestone road that led to Micah's parking place. He stroked her arm, and she stiffened. If she looked at him, even for a moment, she'd dissolve into a puddle of tears.

"I don't want you to break up with me today," he said. "I know you really want to, but you're very emotional right now, and I think you should wait until you have a clear head."

"Our circumstances aren't going to change by waiting," she said.

"Can you wait two days? If you still want to end things by Tuesday, I'll accept your decision. Not happily, but I'll respect it. I'm just asking for a two-day pause before we make anything final."

Katja's chest squeezed hard. Dragging this out for two days would be like taking out stitches from a thick scar before it was properly healed. By yourself, without the assistance of a doctor.

Micah's eyes were soft and pleading.

"I'll still be the moon on Tuesday," she said.

"Maybe not," he responded. "I'm feeling awfully small and cold right now."

If she loved him, she could give him this one last request. And she did love him. Her eyes tightened shut. Why did she let herself fall in love with this man? Stupid, stupid girl!

"Okay," Katja heard herself say. She needed time to find a new place anyway. Somehow she'd get through the next couple days. She felt so weak and worn, she really didn't know how. She needed a miracle.

WORDS OF WISDOM

KATJA FOLLOWED Micah up the stairs to his flat, waiting while he fumbled with the key to the door and then hesitated as she pondered where to go. Staying in Micah's room felt too intimate, even though she slept there alone. Claiming the sofa bed again meant she had nowhere to hide. The formerly locked room was empty, but it had no furniture, unless she was prepared to sleep on the floor. She was exhausted, and that thought didn't appeal to her. She begrudgingly traipsed to Micah's room, closing the door behind her.

She slumped on the bed and pushed her face into her pillow. Only then did she allow the tears to flow. When her heaving stopped and her waterworks had depleted, she slipped into sleep. It was early morning when she awoke with the dusty orange glow of sunrise fading out the dark windows. She was achy from sleeping in her clothes. Her mouth and face felt gross from being unwashed, and she had to go to the bathroom. She could only hope that Micah was still fast asleep and she could sneak down the hall unnoticed.

No such luck. The blue glow of the TV filled the room. Micah reclined bare chested under the covers, leaning against the back of the sofa.

He caught sight of her, and their gaze connected. "Are you hungry?" he asked. "I'll make you breakfast."

She gulped. He looked so appealing. Her heart and mind and physical being wanted him. She was anything but hungry. "No," she muttered. "I'm fine."

She took her time showering. She brushed her teeth and blow-dried her hair. She kept her eyes averted when she stepped determinedly to her room. She couldn't resist a quick look over her shoulder to the living room. The sofa bed was empty. Micah was gone. His absence underscored the loss she felt so deeply already, and a new swirl of grief consumed her.

Katja went back to bed and slept in until almost noon. She could imagine Micah sitting at the table, working on his laptop and waiting for her to wake up, but she really hoped he wasn't. She didn't know how to face him after yesterday, and she wasn't up for another fight.

She needn't have worried. If Micah had returned, he had left again. Maybe he went to church. He did that on Sundays sometimes. They managed to stay clear of each other for the entire day, and on Monday she called Renata and asked if it was possible for her to take a double shift. Fortunately, she said yes. It would keep her out of Micah's flat for the evening, plus she'd make extra money, something she really needed now. She'd scour the papers for a new place to live. Maybe Renata knew of a place somewhere.

She feigned a smile when she entered the coffee shop on Monday morning, not wanting Renata or the other staff to see the sadness that weighed her down. She could fool the others but not her boss.

"Oh, *Schatz*," Renata said as Katja strapped on one of the company aprons. "What happened to the happy girl who left for Berlin with her boyfriend?"

On the word *boyfriend*, Katja's eyes grew red and dumb tears leaked out.

"Come with me," Renata said. She guided her to the small staff room at the back. It was empty and Renata closed the door behind them. "Sit," she said, and Katja did willingly. Her knees were watery, and her whole body felt limp like spaghetti. She had no idea how she was going to stay upright for the rest of the day.

"What happened, *Engel?*" Renata said softly. Her eyes were gentle and kind, and Katja gave into the need to bare her burdens to someone. She told her the whole story of her day in Berlin.

"Better just to end things now, even though it's hard. It would only hurt so much more later on."

"Honey, you've been abandoned by your father, abused by your stepfather, and you've felt rejected by your mother. It's natural that you fear Micah will do the same to you. But has he shown any sign of that? Has he said or done anything to make you believe he feels superior to you?"

Katja paused at that. No, she couldn't really think of anything specific. It was just logical, though. Only a matter of time. "Our stations in life are so different."

"Everyone is equal in God's eyes, my dear."

Everyone may be equal in God's eyes, but they weren't in Frau Sturm's. "You haven't' met his mother. She doesn't like me, and she's very influential in Micah's life."

"You're afraid she'll sway him?"

"Yes." And to help Renata understand more clearly, she described their meeting. "She's a force of nature, Renata, a roaring lion. Compared to her, my mother is a timid mouse who spends all her time cowering in the corner."

"But, what are you?" Renata asked. "What are *you?*"

A tap on the door interrupted them. "Morning rush,

Schatz," Renata said. She patted Katja's hand like the burning questions in her heart had been answered. Had they?

Thankfully, the busyness of the day kept Katja from constantly dwelling on her problems, and even though she felt like a hunchback in the spirit, in the natural she stood tall and wore a friendly face. She labored hard, especially when it was her turn to clean tables and sweep the floor. These physical tasks were minefields for her mind, and she had to work extra hard to keep her thoughts off Micah.

She was in the back putting the cleaning supplies away when she heard Renata's voice.

"Katja, Katja!" Renata pranced toward her with a gorgeous bouquet of flowers in her hand. "These came for you."

Katja froze to the spot. Renata held the flowers out—a mix of red roses, white daisies and sprigs of lavender—and Katja accepted them with a shaky hand. She read the card. "I love you. M."

I love you. His first declaration.

Renata smiled like a mad woman. "You don't have to stay the extra shift, if you don't want to," she said.

Katja smiled shyly. Micah sent her flowers. He told her that he loved her.

"I'll think about it," she said.

WHAT ARE YOU?

KATJA DECIDED NOT to stay for her second shift. She was really lucky that her boss was a diehard romantic. At least when it came to other people. Renata excused her with a pat on the back telling her to go make nice with her handsome boyfriend. Katja smiled at her enthusiasm as she carried the bouquet home.

They were lovely, and the gesture was sweet, but could her objective to end things with Micah be swayed by a collection of flowers? There were bigger issues at stake. What was best for Micah in the long run? What was best for her? Were they the right choice for each other?

She turned her key in the handle of the door of Micah's flat and found it was already unlocked. That was strange. Katja was sure she'd locked it on her way out.

Inside, she set the flowers on the table and went to Micah's room to change out of her black and white uniform. She slipped into a pair of jeans—the only clean ones left were the ones with horizontal tears, exposing sections of her thigh—and her peasant blouse. She decided to keep her hair up in the high pony-tail the way she always wore it for work. The weather had warmed up over the weekend, and the afternoon sun pouring through the windows had heated up the flat.

She wondered what she should say to Micah. What should her position be now? It wasn't just the flowers that had made her waver in her decision to leave, but Micah's note.

Did he really love her?

She already knew beyond a shadow of a doubt that she was hopelessly in love with him. It was the reason her choice was so painful.

Her mind was thoroughly pre-occupied which was why she didn't notice the figure standing in the hall on her way from Micah's room to the bathroom.

Katja jumped back, startled. "Frau Sturm?"

The woman leaned against the frame of the bathroom door. That door had been closed when Katja had passed it the first time. Had Micah's mother been here the whole time? She answered the question for her.

"Don't look so surprised. I have my own key to my son's flat." She added a moment later for emphasis, "too."

"What are you doing here?" Katja finally managed.

"I wanted to see for myself if you were just a visitor like my son claimed." Her eyes cut to the room Katja had just exited. Micah's bedroom. "Or more."

Katja folded her arms in front of her. "And your conclusion?"

"Don't play stupid with me."

"I don't intend to play anything with you."

"Look," Frau Sturm said, tugging on her suit jacket. "We both know what girls like you want from boys like my son."

Katja stiffened. *Girls like her?* "And what would that be?"

"Money."

"I'm not after Micah's money." Katja felt like she'd just walked onto the set of a bad daytime soap opera.

"Oh, please. Look at you! And look at this nice roof

over your head. Be honest. Where did you live before you came here?"

Hot anger boiled in Katja's stomach. How dare this woman?

"Don't bother trying to scramble up a lie. I already know. You slept on the sofa of a flat not leased by you. Before then you lived with your mother and stepfather in a GDR housing project in Berlin. You quit university before you finished your first year."

Katja felt sucker punched.

"So," Frau Sturm continued. "Let's go back to the money. What will it take to get you to leave my son for good? Ten thousand euros? Twenty?"

"Shall I just name my price?" Katja spit out.

"Please do."

"I choose zero euro. Whatever Micah and I have, it has nothing to do with you. I will not be bullied or bribed. Believe it or not, money can't buy you everything."

"Mother?"

They both gasped at the sight of Micah standing at the end of the hall. Katja's heart stammered. How much had he heard?

"Micah, *Schatz*, hello." Frau Sturm pulled her face into a friendly smile like she hadn't just been caught belittling the girl in the hall. Her stilettos clicked on the floor as she moved to her son and kissed his cheeks. He stood still, not returning her affection.

"I think you should leave," he said.

Katja couldn't tell if he was talking to his mother or to her. She stepped back toward the bedroom. Micah caught her eye. "Not you."

He guided his mother to the front door. Katja could hear their muffled voices from her position in the hall.

Frau Sturm switched to English. "This is a mistake."

"Then it's my mistake."

"She's just like…"

"Mother!"

"And what is that thing in her lip?"

Katja scowled and pulled her lip ring into her mouth with her teeth. She was tempted to storm out past the two of them and make a big scene, but a part of her didn't want to give in to Frau Bully.

The door shut loudly, and in the next moment Micah was back, staring at her again, an apologetic expression on his face.

"I'm sorry about that."

"She hates me."

"She doesn't know you. She's just really protective of me."

Katja rolled her eyes.

"I bought groceries," he said. "Can I make you dinner?"

"Micah."

"It's not Tuesday yet. If you leave tomorrow, this will be our last night. At least have dinner with me."

Micah's eyes were so kind and pleading. Katja felt her anger melt a little. "You've made dinner for me so many times."

"You're right," he said. "It's your turn to make it."

She snorted. "Do you have a death wish?"

"No, actually. And I'd like to see you live another day as well. I think you need a lesson."

She folded her arms and leaned against the wall. "You think you can teach me to cook?"

He cocked his head. "I'd like to try."

CULINARY ARTS

KATJA COULDN'T RESIST Micah's charms and had, against her better judgment, agreed to the cooking lesson. What she needed was to hide away from Micah, to somehow escape the undeniable pull he had on her. Instead, she'd just signed up for more emotional torture.

She was her own worst enemy.

Micah scooped up the remote and turned on a satellite radio station that played soft jazz. Katja silently moaned. Romantic music? She really was in trouble.

She followed Micah into the kitchen where he turned on the taps and washed his hands. He offered her the soap. She tried to keep her distance, but there was only one tap, and Micah didn't seem to be in any hurry to finish rinsing his hands. She kept a good half meter between them and stubbornly waited until he left his position by the sink. "What are you going to teach me to make?"

"Something simple. Pasta with braised vegetables and sheep cheese."

"Well, we both know I'm lousy at cooking pasta. What's the big secret?"

Micah smirked. "Slow down, young chef. One thing at a time." He opened a cupboard door. "First, you need the right pot. Uncooked pasta must have room to expand. You want to cover it with water without filling it more than three-quarters full. You don't want it to boil over."

Hmm. That was one of her problems. She obviously didn't use the right pot, or enough water. Good to know.

Micah handed her the pot, and she filled it, and placed it on the stove, turning the element to high. "Where's the pasta?"

Micah removed a package from his grocery bag. "It's here, but you don't want to add it until the water's boiling. In the meantime, we can wash and slice the vegetables." Micah produced a small amount of fresh mushrooms, a zucchini and a package of grape tomatoes. Katja washed them and returned them to the cutting board.

The kitchen wasn't that big, and Katja found it difficult to move without brushing against Micah at times.

"I'm sorry," she muttered.

He stared down at her. "Please, don't be."

She started slicing the zucchini at the thickness Micah had shown her. Being in close quarters like this might be torture, but she appreciated the lesson. No one had taken the time to teach her how to cook before.

"Now we'll sauté the zucchini and mushrooms in butter," Micah said while scooping a spoonful of butter into a frying pan. "Turn it on medium, and throw them in."

Katja did as instructed, scraping the sliced vegetables from the cutting board into the pan.

"You just need to keep stirring them so they don't burn."

Katja nodded and gave the vegetables a whirl. "What about the tomatoes?"

"Those go on top, later. Fresh, not cooked." Micah

pulled a bottle of wine out of one of the bags. "For the lady." He opened it and poured Katja a glass.

She raised an eyebrow. "You were pretty certain I'd say yes to this invitation?"

He shrugged while pouring himself a glass of sparkling water. "I figured I had a fifty-fifty chance."

The frying pan sizzled and Micah instructed, "Keep stirring."

Katja did as told. "Can I ask you something?"

"Sure."

"Did your mother like Greta?"

Micah paused until she looked at him. "No, she didn't. If that makes you feel better. My mother is always rude."

It did, in fact, make her feel better. She was glad to know she wasn't the only one on the receiving end of Frau Sturm's disapproval.

"The water's ready for the pasta," Micah said. He opened the bag and handed it to Katja. "You may do the honors."

Katja smiled, despite herself, and poured the contents in. "How long do you cook it?"

"About ten minutes," Micah said. He checked the package and nodded. "Italians like to undercook it by three minutes and then cook it with the sauce for the remaining three. The pasta captures the flavors of the sauce, that way."

Katja was impressed. "How did you learn to cook?" She couldn't imagine his mother stepping foot into a kitchen.

"We had professional cooks. I wanted to learn, so they taught me."

He had cooks. She had a mother who could barely pull herself out of bed.

"It helps to set a timer," Micah added, winking. "Especially if you find yourself distracted by a song demanding to be written or a picture insisting on being sketched." He set the timer and then handed her a spoon. "You need to stir it once in a while."

Micah pulled the foil lid off a small plastic container. "Now to add crème and a bit of salt and pepper to the vegetables."

Katja found it increasingly difficult to pull her gaze away from her teacher. Men who knew their way around a kitchen were titillating. Her pulse jumped as she watched him, and she felt herself flush. "So, what's left?" she asked, trying to distract herself.

"The cheese. Many people like Parmesan, but I prefer sheep cheese. It adds a nice tang." He sliced a piece off the block and handed it to Katja. "You can grate it."

Micah produced a grater, and Katja began the process of shredding the cheese onto a plate. Micah made no attempt to hide the fact he was staring at her.

"Don't do that," she said.

"Do what?"

"You know what."

"I want to kiss you."

She dropped the cheese and dared to glance at him. "I don't think that's a good idea."

He stepped closer, forcing her to back up against the counter. "I think it's a great idea."

Oh, Lord, she really wanted him to kiss her, but it was still a really, really bad idea. Her pulse raged, and her body flooded with warmth. Her throat grew dry. Maybe just one kiss. She heard herself say, "Perhaps it's not the worst idea you've ever had."

Yes it was! What was she thinking? It was a terrible, terrible idea!

He pressed his mouth to her ear, his breath causing

tremors that would break the Richter scale. "Admit it. It's an incredible idea."

She gulped, wanting nothing more than to grab him by the shirt and pull him to her. "Maybe it's not so bad," she whispered.

"Not so bad works for me." Micah's lips found hers, and Katja was sure the kitchen floor had cracked open. She was falling, helpless. She grabbed his head and returned the kiss, urgently taking him in.

Then she remembered her oath to leave.

She'd told him he had until Tuesday to change her mind, and here she was madly kissing him on Monday night.

Did she have no willpower at all? Had she changed her mind about what she should do so easily? Tomorrow, she'd still be the poor girl chasing a dream, and he'd still be the rich boy with every advantage. And with a domineering mother who scared the crap out of her. Frau Sturm would always be trying to break them up, and eventually she would win. She and Micah had too much working against them.

She had to be stronger than this.

She placed a palm against his chest and pushed gently. "Micah…"

He tapped a finger to her lips. "You promised me until Tuesday."

"That's tomorrow."

"Then I have you until tomorrow."

She quivered under his touch. She would leave tomorrow, but she knew beyond a doubt that Micah would have her heart for much longer. She ran fingers along the roughness of his jaw, drank in his face, his eyes, the curls on his head. She was memorizing him. Something told her she'd be living in this moment forever.

"I love you, Katja."

Her heart stopped. Then she kissed him again and didn't quit until the timer went.

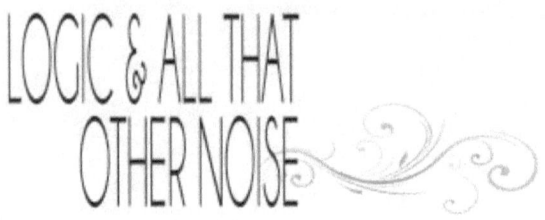

LOGIC & ALL THAT OTHER NOISE

T<small>HEY</small> <small>ATE</small> dinner by candlelight and spent the night curled up together on the sofa bed. Micah remained in control, and she was glad he'd enforced a slow pace. Especially since she still didn't know if staying with him was the right thing to do.

Tuesday arrived, and even though she went through the motions of packing, she didn't leave. It wasn't a clear win for Micah, and they both knew it. Despite their passion, Katja wasn't convinced she'd made the right choice, yet the longer she stayed the deeper she sank. By the weekend, she knew she was a prisoner to Micah, no matter what his rules were, no matter how torn her heart would be when the end came.

Saturday brought a welcome diversion from her emotional torment in the form of Jonas's art festival. It was held outdoors at the foot of the pedestrian zone called *Neustädter Markt* by the Golden Horseman statue. Katja had gotten hired to play music on a small stage while people meandered through the artwork and crafts displayed there.

It was within walking distance from their flat, and Micah insisted on carrying her guitar. "It makes me feel cool," he joked.

Katja laughed. "It makes you look cool."

He purposefully bumped into her. "Then I'll just have to carry it for you all the time."

It was a warm, sunny day with clear blue skies, and the fair was full of people taking in the show. Jonas waved her over when he saw her.

"Hey, Jonas," she said. "How's it going?"

"Pretty good." Jonas beamed his boyish grin. "Already sold one painting."

"That's great," Katja said. She motioned to Micah. "This is …" Again, she didn't know what to call him and settled for just his name. "Micah."

They shook hands and Katja looked around for Renata. "Is your mother here?"

"Not yet. She'll stop by later."

Katja took a moment to look at Jonas's work before setting up. "He's good," she said to Micah. He nodded his head. "Who knew there were so many talented people in the world?" He squeezed her shoulders. "Here I thought you were the only one."

She swatted his arm. "You're such a sap."

He laughed. "Do you need any help?"

"It's just me and my guitar. I think I can manage, but thanks."

The small stage had a sound system set up. The guy managing it ran her through a short sound check. "It's all yours," he said.

"I'm going to be here a while," Katja said to Micah.

"I'll have a look around and then go home," he said. "We'll meet up later?"

She nodded and took the stage, sitting on the stool provided there. She'd play mostly instrumentals, unless a group gathered wanting to listen to her sing. She was fine either way. She smiled as she watched Jonas chatting up admirers of his work. Though young and geeky looking, he had a self-confidence and charm that would go a long way. Renata had done a good job.

Micah caught her eye and pointed at a canvas. Katja nodded and mouthed, *It's good*. Micah smiled and surprised her by picking it up and handing several bills to Jonas.

She watched as he walked away with a new painting under his arm. She loved that he supported Jonas by purchasing one.

She loved *him*.

It was true. She was hopelessly snared. Ignoring the truth wouldn't change it. She felt surprisingly light about her admission. A smile threatened to take over her face. She chewed on her lip ring and tried to stay focused on her playing.

She spotted another familiar face in the crowd. Maurice was there, checking out the pottery. It was strange to see him around town milling about. She only ever saw him at the Blue Note. He followed the music and eventually spotted the source. He drew closer.

"*Ma Cherie*," he called out. "I should've known it was you. You play exquisitely."

She laughed and blew him a kiss.

If only Renata were here. She'd love to introduce them. Maurice and Renata had become two of her most favorite people.

Katja finished her two-hour set and collected her pay. Micah wasn't home when she got back, and she felt the emptiness. He hadn't mentioned his plans for the day, only that they'd meet up later. She put her guitar away and rested on the sofa.

The art show had inspired her so she pulled her sketch pad out. Her eyes were drawn to the sketch of Micah that hung on the formerly locked door. She lifted herself from her cross-legged position on the sofa and carefully removed the drawing, taking it into the bathroom where she stood staring at her image in the mirror.

She poised her pencil over the shadowy area beside the drawing of Micah's head and began to rapidly pencil in the lines of her face. She made her eyes bright and her mouth turned up with amusement. Her image looked mischievous and happy, her gaze directed at Micah.

She propped up the sketch and stood back to examine it. Yes, it said what she wanted it to say, that she admired and adored him. She signed it: *I love you, K*, and hung it back up on the door.

She fell asleep on the sofa and awoke to Micah lifting her legs and sitting down under them.

"Hey, sleepyhead," he said. He took one of her feet and rubbed it.

"Oh, that feels good."

"I knew you were keeping me around for something." He switched to the other one.

"I thought you were keeping me around."

Her eyes darted to the revised sketch on the wall, and Micah followed her gaze. He slipped out from under her, walked over to view it and tilted his head. His hand went to his chin and he rubbed the shadow of his beard. "Hmm. It's charming, yet bold. The artist has a way with a pencil, crafting shadow and light. Brilliant, actually."

Katja laughed at Micah's poor attempt at mimicking an art critic. "I'm glad you like it."

His dark, simmering gaze locked with hers. "I don't just like it. I *love* it."

Katja blushed and pursed her lips to suppress a girlish giggle.

Micah returned and pulled her up onto his lap. His lips brushed against her ear and he whispered, "I think you should kiss me now. Kiss me good."

She reached for his face, tracing his jaw with her fingertip, and met his lips with hers. They were warm and soft, and she trembled as his tongue played with her lip ring. He ran his fingers lightly over her temples, and she responded in kind, holding his head, and running fingers through his curls. She pulled back to gaze at his face and lost herself in the love she saw there. Then she tucked herself under his arm, feeling safe and secure—something she hadn't felt in a very long time.

"Are you getting hungry?" he asked.

"A little."

"I'm starved. Let's start dinner."

They'd been cooking together since her first lesson, and every night Micah taught her something new.

"What's on the menu tonight?" she asked.

"Something simple. Mushroom soup. Just add water."

Micah paused at the table and picked up the fruit bowl that was nearly overflowing with coins and bills from Katja's earnings. "This is not your usual center piece." He handed it to Katja. "Please take this to your bank."

Katja shook her head. "It's my contribution to the rent."

"Katja, I have enough money. I had no problem paying the rent before you came."

"What about groceries?"

"I also ate before you came. And you don't exactly eat that much. Besides, I prefer your company to eating alone. You're doing me a favor."

Katja sighed and accepted the bowl. "Thank you."

Micah smiled. "No problem. I need somewhere to put the fruit."

MATCHMAKING

KATJA HAD the morning shift the next day and she made sure to leave with enough time to get there early. She enjoyed having time to make small talk with Renata before jumping into the fray of taking orders, foaming milk, cleaning the display case and wiping tables. She loved the aroma that hit her face as she walked in the door. Sweet scents of sugar and cinnamon combined with the stronger, stark aroma of rich, fresh brewed coffee.

She greeted Renata as she tied on her apron. "I missed seeing you yesterday."

"It was so busy here. I couldn't get away until later. You were already gone when I arrived, but Jonas said you were wonderful."

"Your son's a good artist," Katja said.

"And a good person," Renata added. "That is the most important thing." She clasped Katja's hand. "And how are you?"

Katja had shared some details about the disastrous trip to Berlin and her following encounter with Micah's antagonistic mother. Renata was also aware of her cautious reconciliation with Micah.

Katja smiled reassuringly. "Things are fine. Good really."

"Ah, I'm so glad."

"How are things with you?"

"Always the same." Renata rolled her eyes. "Nothing is ever new with me, *Schatz*."

Maybe it was time to change that.

"Renata?"

"Yes?"

"There's an open mic night at the Blue Note tomorrow. I might play a song or two. You should come."

Renata pulled back and stared at Katja with wide eyes. "I don't think so."

"Why not? It would be fun. It would be *new*."

"I have to work."

"Renata, you're the *boss*. You can give yourself time off. Besides," Katja resisted the conniving smile that wanted to lift up her lips, "you never know who you might meet." Like a charming French bachelor, maybe.

Renata's brows furrowed into a V. "Are you trying to set me up?"

"No, no," Katja said too quickly. "Of course not. I just meant, I could introduce you to some of my friends."

Renata cocked her head. "Meet your friends?"

"And hear music. You do like music, don't you?"

"Of course. Who doesn't like music?"

"Then come with me. Live a little, Renata." She waved an arm at the shop. "You have to admit you could use a change of scenery."

Renata's lips twitched, considering. "Okay, *Schatze*. But just because I'm very fond of you."

Katja smiled and gave her a quick hug. "Awesome."

Katja waited near the entrance of the Blue Note for Renata like they'd agreed. Micah had to work late, so he promised to join her later. Katja checked the time on her phone and frowned. Renata was late. Katja hoped she hadn't changed her mind and bailed without letting her know.

She smiled as other people passed by to enter the club, stepping out of the way, trying not to feel strange about loitering on the sidewalk alone. She stretched her neck, peering down the darkening street. The streetlights flickered on and cast shadows against the four-story stone buildings that lined the narrow road. Her eyes ran across the peeling posters on the wall across from her—band advertisements, festivals and markets. Some coming soon, some long past.

A woman rounded the corner dressed in jeans and a casual, billowing blouse. Her very *insensible* shoes clacked on the cobblestone street as she crossed the road. She waved to Katja with a bemused grin.

Katja's mouth went slack. She barely recognized her friend. Instead of being pulled back in a low ponytail like she wore it every day at the coffee shop, her shoulder-length, salt and pepper hair hung in soft waves around her face. She wore a little eye makeup and peach-colored lipstick.

"Renata! You look fantastic!"

"Thanks. It's been a while since I put in the effort. I feel a little self-conscious."

"Well, you don't look it. You're the epitome of confidence."

Katja linked arms with Renata and opened the door to the Blue Note to lead her in.

Maurice stood at his usual place behind the bar. He had that teddy-bear look, rounder in the belly and cheeks, but he had a nice face and a friendly smile. He greeted Katja warmly when she walked in. "*Ma Cherie*! Good to see you!"

"You too, Maurice. I want to introduce you to my friend, Renata Beck. She's also my boss and the owner of the coffee shop near my building."

He held out a broad hand, and Renata shook it. "Nice to meet you," he said. His eyes sparkled with sincerity, and Katja was satisfied to see that Renata responded by blushing.

"Nice to meet you, too," she said.

"Are you up?" Maurice asked Katja. She nodded, and added her name to the list. Maurice left to talk to Holger who was setting up the sound for the open mic night.

"So he's the reason you wanted me to come?" Renata asked.

"No, I mean, sure, but also to hear the music," Katja said. "Right?"

"Well, little miss matchmaker, don't get your hopes up," Renata responded with a grin and a shake of the head.

"Why? You're both respectable, likable and *eligible*. You both own your own drinking establishments. And you both like to use pet names. Granted, yours are more varied."

"Hardly grounds for a relationship."

"Fine. But they're great grounds for a friendship. You could be friends couldn't you?"

"Oh, *ma Cherie*," Renata mimicked. "You are a worse romantic than I am."

Maurice returned and they ordered drinks. Katja excused herself conveniently with the guise that she had to use the ladies room. When she returned she chuckled. Her instincts were right. Maurice and Renata were in a close huddle, conversing animatedly over the noise of the chattering patrons and the music pumping in from the stereo.

She mentally reviewed her to-do list. Renata + Maurice. Check.

THE SURPRISE

ONCE KATJA DECIDED to let herself be happy, she was very, very happy. She and Micah went on long walks and romantic picnics. They told stories and laughed. They hugged and kissed, and kissed some more. They cuddled on the sofa bed and watched romantic movies while eating candy and chocolates.

She had a spring to her step and a smile plastered on her face. She constantly watched the clock, counting the minutes until Micah came home from work, resuming her place on the steps while she waited for him to round the corner.

Renata gently teased her at work. "*Schatz*, you will blow out the windows with your joy."

"Let's go out for dinner tonight," Micah said on a Saturday morning. He pulled Katja close and kissed her neck. She groaned, stretching out for more.

"I'm thinking high end," he added between kisses. "Dress in something nice."

Katja straightened and pulled back. "I don't have anything *high end* and *nice*." He *knew* that.

"Such a sad situation, tsk, tsk." His eyes lighted with a humor she didn't share. "Oh, come on, let me take you shopping."

This kind of thing just reminded Katja of why she'd been tempted to break up with him in the first place. She wasn't a sophisticated fashionista like his mother or his friend, Anna, from the bank. She felt herself shrinking back. "I don't know."

"Please, Katja. This isn't a sun and moon thing," Micah persisted. "It's just a thing." He smiled encouragingly. "It'll be fun."

She hated shopping. "For who?"

He smirked. "For me!"

Katja reluctantly relented and quickly grabbed her purse. If he thought she'd change out of her torn jeans just to impress the fancy dress shop workers, he had another thing coming. He opened the door and followed her out, and Katja got the distinct impression he was enjoying the view of her behind by the way he chuckled.

She shot him a look over her shoulder. "Stop that!" She tried to sound stern, but she could hear the smile in her voice.

Micah laughed. "What?"

He took her to a swanky shop in the center of the old town, a place Katja would never have stepped foot in on her own.

Micah helped to sort through the dresses despite the clerk's thinly veiled disapproval, and she tried on a number of them, showcasing each one for him. If she could judge by the look on his face, he liked what he saw. She was aghast when she checked the price tags, but Micah swiped playfully at her hands, telling her not to worry. He bought her casual clothes, too: jeans and blouses, and a short, fun sundress.

Katja wasn't used to having brand new clothes. She wondered if deep down Micah was trying to change her, and it stirred up feelings of doubt.

But the clothes *were* nice.

"You're spoiling me," she said.

"I want to spoil you. You deserve to have nice things." He quickly added, "And that doesn't mean I'm trying to change you." Micah continued to prove his knack for mind reading. Or maybe he really did know and understand her.

"But," he continued. "I *do* have money, and I do like to spend it on, well, *you*. So don't try to *change* me by trying to stop me."

Touché.

She gripped his hand, stood on her tiptoes, and kissed his cheek. "Thank you."

They went back to Micah's flat to change and get ready. Katja chose the shimmery, little black dress. She examined her image in the bedroom mirror. With silver, strapped heels, and her hair piled in a messy up-do, she could easily pass for one of those uptown girls.

When Micah checked in on her, his eyes popped, and his jaw slacked. Then he whistled. "Simply beautiful." He grabbed her hand and tugged her, snapping her body to his. He rested his forehead on hers and inhaled.

"You smell amazing." His lips made a butterfly trail from her temple, over her cheekbone and to her lips as his hands explored her curves. She quivered under his touch, every neuron in her body resounding with a loud *yes*!

He kissed the base of her neck in a way that made her knees give out. They fell on the bed, and she almost exploded. They kissed with a passion Katja had never experienced before.

Still, there was a line Micah was not willing to cross. He ducked his head in the crook of her neck and took several long breaths. Then he pressed up on his elbow and stared at her. He ran a finger along her brow, pushing hair off her face.

"You are so beautiful." He kissed her forehead again. "But we have reservations."

She laughed. "I think I have to do my hair over."

He helped her off the bed. "Get to it then. We don't want to be late."

He took her to dinner at a place that had valet parking, chandeliers hanging from the ceiling, and more cutlery around the plates than Katja knew what to do with. It was lovely and the dining experience, delightful. This was a life she could get used to, she supposed.

Micah's eyes never left her face. She blushed under his scrutiny.

"You're making me nervous."

"I can't help it. You are so exquisitely stunning. All the guys in this place are sneaking looks, and half the ladies, too."

He smiled warmly and she smiled in return.

Then he did something that made her heart stop. Micah stood, and suddenly he was kneeling beside her, a little black box appearing like magic in the palm of his hand. Her mind knew what was going on. She *did* watch American movies. But her heart refused to restart. She was certain she would faint. At the very least, she didn't think she could stop herself from gaping unattractively. Her hand clasped over her mouth, and tears welled up behind her eyes.

"Katja Stoltz, will you do me the honor of being my wife?"

Katja stared hard at him, unable to make her lips move. "Yes," she finally mustered. Then she burst out laughing. "Yes! A million times yes!"

The crowd in the restaurant cheered, and Katja threw herself into Micah's arms.

"I love you," he said.

"I love you, too."

They kissed tenderly and then pressed each other away, keenly aware of the audience they'd acquired. They fed each other chocolate dessert, and Micah ordered Katja a glass of her favorite red wine. She ogled her ring finger, delighting in how the candlelight reflected off the diamond.

They giggled like school children, and made plans.

"Since you've obviously been thinking about this," Katja said. "Do you have a date in mind?"

"How does tomorrow sound?"

She playfully smacked his hand. "Seriously?"

He smiled crookedly. "I am serious, but, I concede it might take a little while to get a dress and all that. I'm okay with something small, unless you want big. Anything you want, Katja. Anything."

"Small is good," she said. She really didn't have anyone to invite other than her family and a couple childhood friends, Renata and Maurice, of course, and the few friends she'd made since moving to Dresden.

She frowned. "Does your mother know?"

Micah reached across the table and cupped her hands with both of his. "She's well aware. I won't lie and say she's delighted, but she's coming around. At the end of the day, she just wants me to be happy. And *you* make me happy."

And he made her happy. Extremely happy. Katja

couldn't remember a time when she felt so joyous, so giddy. One day soon she would be Frau Micah Sturm!

After dinner, she leaned against Micah as he helped her back to the car park. She wasn't used to walking in heels, and she gladly took the opportunity to be assisted by Micah. She waved her diamond ring under the street-lamps, stopping to *ooh* and *ahh* over the gem as it sparkled in the light.

It was a short drive to their flat.

Their flat!

It was the first time Katja had thought of the flat as anything but Micah's. Surely it was time for his room to be their room, too. A thrill of excitement charged up her spine. Their passionate preamble to the evening had only been an appetizer.

They walked from the car toward the apartment building, hand in hand, stopping every few steps to kiss and giggle. She couldn't peel her eyes off his face.

That was why he saw *her* before she did.

Sitting on *their* steps.

A woman with long, wavy, sandy blond hair.

All the blood drained from Katja's head, and her legs nearly gave out. She held onto Micah's arm for dear life.

Greta.

A CHANGE OF PLANS

GRETA'S EYES scanned Katja from head to toe, and then zeroed in on Micah. "I see you have a type."

Micah's face had lost all color, his eyes wide like he was seeing a ghost. He *was*, and so was Katja.

Greta approached, and Micah gestured to Katja without looking away from the lost girl's face. "Wait for me inside."

Katja didn't want to leave him alone with her. "Micah?"

"I'll be in in a minute." He waved her off, but it felt like a slap in the face. Greta was there, and she was dismissed.

Her legs trembled as she went up the steps, but once inside, she slipped off her heels and raced to their flat at the top. Her hand shook as she fussed with the key to unlock the door. She ran to the living room window and looked down at the sidewalk below.

Micah and Greta stood face to face a quarter-meter apart. He threw his hands about, saying something passionately. She put palms out to calm him. Their lips moved and Katja wished desperately she could hear what they were saying.

She hoped he was telling Greta about her, how he'd moved on and fallen in love with someone else. She hoped

Greta would walk away, a final goodbye, and that Micah would look for her in the window and give her an encouraging smile.

Her heart dropped when they started walking down the street, side by side.

No, wait! Where are you going? Katja's lungs burned as she watched, the back of Micah's curly head and Greta's long hair flowing down to her waist. It could've been Katja and Micah. The similarities between Greta and her were striking. And terrifying.

They disappeared around the corner, and Katja's heart ripped in half. She collapsed into a chair.

They wouldn't be gone for long, would they? Micah wouldn't leave her waiting. Of course not. He loved her. He wanted to marry her.

Greta was my first serious girlfriend. I would've married her.

Micah had loved her once. He'd *slept* with her. They had a history.

Greta.

What was *she* doing here? Why wasn't she *dead*?

Not that Katja wished anyone dead. She just didn't want her fiancé's ex to show up on the same night they'd agreed to be married. A low groan erupted from her belly. That woman had a way of ruining everything, and Katja hadn't even said one word to her.

She dragged herself to Micah's room, and tore her dress off in a huff. She pulled on a pair of yoga pants and a T-shirt and returned to the living room window, her eyes searching.

He just needed a few answers. He was in shock. She could understand that. He needed some time to process this twist of fate and sort through his emotions.

But, he'd come back to her, right? He'd remember they

were celebrating the beginning of their life together and come back to her.

Where was he?

Finally, when the anguish of not knowing where he was and what he was doing became too great, she tried calling and then texting, but he didn't respond.

The hollowness in her being was spreading. She wanted to believe in him. She had to give him the benefit of the doubt. Soon he'd be bounding up the stairwell, back to her.

Like it always did in moments of extreme emotion, her guitar called to her. She unclicked the case and gathered it into her arms, caressing it gently. She strummed a melancholy chord, letting the simple beauty of the music soothe her. As the minutes ticked by and then the hours, words started to come.

Don't go now
I know it's late and the light is growing dim
But I just like the way
You feel beside me on the front steps, not yet
Sing me one more song,
The one about the girl who finds the whole wide world

She stopped picking and put the pen down. Did she just hear footsteps in the stairwell? She waited. Nothing. The pain in her heart deepened, her sadness consuming her until she couldn't bear it anymore. The aching, empty hurt gradually morphed into anger.

Where was he? She was going to kill him when he got home. Right after she knocked off his ex. She knew she shouldn't have let her guard down. She knew she was stupid to believe a boy like Micah could love a girl like her.

Stupid, stupid, stupid.

And as quickly as the anger flared, it melted and the sorrow returned. Tears streamed down her face. Her sadness was thick and heavy like an entity of its own.

Don't go now
I know it's late and the dark is folding in
But I just like the way
Your fingers close around my hand, so grand
And sing me one more song
The one about the girl who finds the whole wide world

The black sky turned deep purple, then bruised blue. Black birds cawed as the morning dawned. She fiddled with her ring, choking back the tears. Immense pain and anger wrenched her soul. How could he do this to her? How could he so easily leave her for Greta?

Katja's first instincts about Micah were right. He hadn't moved on. She'd merely been a replacement for the person he really wanted, the person he thought he'd never find.

She wept hard and long until every bone and muscle hurt as much as her heart, using up all the tissues in the box. She didn't throw them in the trash, but left the messy pile like a bitter monument for Micah to find when he finally returned. She packed up her guitar and her bag, and tossed her ring into the fruit bowl before leaving.

Katja wished she'd never met Micah Sturm.

RUNNING

Katja's first impulse was to run to the coffee shop, but it wasn't open yet. Maybe it was a good thing. Saying goodbye to Renata would be too hard. She couldn't bear even one more gram of pain.

She kept walking, her mind in a fuzzy daze, and she hadn't even realized where her legs had taken her until she arrived at the door of the Blue Note. She pulled on the handle, but it didn't budge. Of course the establishment was closed, too, this early in the morning. She collapsed on the steps and let her head fall into her hands. Her face was wet, and she wiped it with her sleeve.

Suddenly, she was exhausted. Not sleeping a wink overnight and getting your heart stomped on would do that. She rested her head against the door and closed her eyes. Within minutes she was sleeping. Her dreams were a mashup of the day: shopping with Micah, dinner, his proposal. Her subconscious wanted to hold on to those memories, to hold on to Micah. Greta's face would flash, and she'd cry out and pull back the restaurant scene so she could listen to Micah's declaration of love once again.

But she couldn't fight the nightmare that followed: Greta and Micah under the streetlamp, walking away. Greta glancing back and shooting her a wicked look, like a shard of glass stabbing Katja in the chest, stealing her very breath.

Her eyes snapped open.

"Katja?"

Maurice stood over her, a frown filling his round face. Katja blinked. Her mind was so busy torturing her, for a second she didn't remember why she was sitting on Maurice's steps.

Then she did. It wasn't just a bad dream. The whole thing was horribly real. A new lump filled her throat, and she had to work to swallow.

Maurice reached for her hand and helped her to her feet. "What happened, *ma Cherie*?"

Katja opened her mouth but the words didn't come. It was too painful to speak the truth of what had happened aloud.

"I'm here to say goodbye," she finally managed.

"You're leaving?"Maurice asked, his frown growing deeper. "But why?"

Katja worked to control her features. She must flatten out the pain. She didn't want to blurt out what a fool she had been to anyone, but especially not to someone she respected. Besides, one word about it and she'd turn into a blubbering mess.

"It's just time," she said.

Maurice shifted awkwardly. "Come in for a drink first. I'm talking orange juice, though I have a feeling you really could use something stronger."

"You're a prophet. Add a cup of coffee and you're on."

Katja sat on a bar stool she'd sat on dozens of times and took in the shadowy pub with fondness. This was where she got her sea legs as an artist, where she tried out her new songs and developed confidence to keep playing. It was where she had introduced Renata to Maurice and watched their affection take root and grow. It was where she and Micah…

No, she wouldn't think of him. She shook her head, as if that would rid him from her thoughts.

Maurice provided a glass of juice and a cup of coffee. "On the house," he said, concern still deeply etched on his round face.

She gulped back the juice, her throat parched from weeping. "Thank you. And thanks for everything else, too."

"Like what?"

"Like letting me play here. For believing in me."

"That part was easy, *ma Cherie*. You're very talented. And beautiful. And smart. As they like to say, you have the whole package."

She grimaced. A lot of good it had done her. She finished her coffee while watching Maurice clean the bar. He didn't pry, and she was thankful.

"Please say goodbye to Renata for me," she said.

"Are you sure you don't want to tell her yourself?" he asked gently. "She's very fond of you."

Katja knew Renata was already at the coffee shop but it was too close to Micah's flat. She couldn't risk running into him.

"I know, and I'm very fond of her. It's just, I have to go right now. I'm so sorry I can't tell her in person, but I'll call her. Tell her I'll call her later, okay?"

"Of course." Maurice threw a tea towel over his shoulder. "We'll miss you here."

Katja forced a smile. "I'll miss you, too."

She picked up her guitar and bag, and pushed on the front door.

"Wait!" Maurice called after her. "Where are you going?"

Katja shrugged. "Wherever the next train is headed."

DON'T GO NOW

THE PARKING LOT of the train station was filled with bicycles owned by people who rode their bikes to the station in order to catch a train to work. Katja cut through it, jig sawing her way, struggling with the weight and bulkiness of her baggage.

She entered through the tall, wide doors into the bright, busy building. The ceilings were high, peaking with a glass pyramid-like topper, echoing the sounds of footsteps and chatter in many languages: German, French, Polish, English to name a few. The perimeter was lined with food kiosks and book stores, and on another day, she might've taken time to peruse the selection, of both the food and the books. Instead, she went directly to the ticket center and stood in line. When she reached the front, the attendant asked her where she wanted to go.

"Where is the next train headed?"

The clerk checked the schedule. "There's one leaving in fifteen minutes for Berlin, and one ten minutes later to Frankfurt."

Frankfurt or Berlin? Frankfurt would be a clean start. She didn't know anyone there. She also didn't know her way around. It would be starting over from scratch, and she didn't know if she had the energy for that. Berlin, the city, was still home. And truth be told, she deeply missed her mother and sister. Suddenly, she needed their comfort.

"Berlin."

"One way or return."

"One way."

She went directly to the platform stated on her ticket and waited. The chairs were all occupied, so she leaned against a cement post. The sadness weighed heavily in her cheeks, making the bones of her face ache, and her eyelids felt heavy and hooded. She just wanted to lie down and sleep, but that would have to wait until she got to Berlin.

Time seemed to drag. Again, she checked the large, white clock that hung in the middle of the platform: ten more minutes.

"Katja! Katja!"

Her eyes popped wide open. Was she seeing things?

Micah stood on the platform on the other side of the tracks.

"Katja!" he shouted again. "Don't go! Please, wait!"

Katja's heart thumped against her chest. A train arrived on Micah's side of the tracks, blocking her view of him. She stood still, feeling paralyzed. The train left, and she searched for Micah but he was gone.

She folded her arms tightly around her chest. Maybe she'd imagined it. She was sleep deprived and emotionally distraught. Her mind was playing evil tricks on her. She glanced up at the clock again: five minutes.

Come on. She was so tired. She just needed to leave this place and start over. No more Dresden. No more Micah Sturm.

"Katja!"

She turned, and he was there. Right in front of her. She wasn't imagining it.

"Go away," she said.

Three more minutes.

"Please, Katja, hear me out."

"You chose her over me. Now go away."

"I didn't choose her. I'm choosing you. I want you."

Katja felt her lip quiver. "You left with her."

"I had to hear her story. Please understand."

"You didn't answer your phone."

"She took it from me and wouldn't give it back until she was done talking."

"You didn't have to stay with her. It was our engagement night. You spent it with her!"

"I had to know, Katja. I'm so sorry. I was just so stunned to see her after so long. And I had to know why."

One minute.

"Did you kiss her?"

"What?"

She knew he'd heard her. "Did you kiss her?"

His hesitation was her answer. She turned away and he grabbed her arm. "Just a goodbye kiss. That's all."

She narrowed her unforgiving gaze at him. "At least you got that from one of us."

Thirty seconds.

Her phone rang. She fumbled to remove it from her purse. "Katja Stoltz." Her frown deepened. "Sibylle, calm down... Oh my God... Okay, stay home. Just lock the door. I'm actually at the train station. I'll be there soon."

"What is it?" Micah asked.

She glared at him. "Horst beat up my mother."

His expression darkened. Did his mind go to the same place hers did? That it was his fault?

The train pulled up, and the doors opened in front of Katja. She picked up her bag with one hand and her guitar with the other, conveniently making it impossible for her to hug Micah, or worse, for him to reach out for her.

"Katja?"

She hardened her heart to spare herself more pain. "Bye, Micah," she muttered. She boarded the train and never looked back.

SURVIVING

HER PHONE BUZZED REPEATEDLY in her pocket, each time like a branding iron in her side. She knew who it was, and she didn't want to talk to him. How could she talk when she could barely breathe? He'd maimed and injured her soul, tearing it to pieces.

But, maybe it was Sibylle? The thought forced her to check her phone—his phone—and to feel freshly wounded every time she saw his name. When she refused to answer his calls, he switched to texts.

I shouldn't have gone with her. I'm sorry. Please, can we talk?

I know you're mad, and I don't blame you. I was a jerk. Just talk to me!

Katja, I love you.

She powered it off. If Micah really loved her, he wouldn't have gone with Greta. He could've made plans to meet her the next day, or the next week if all he needed to do was to satisfy his curiosity. At the very least, he should've come home before dawn.

The glaring fact was he'd made a choice, and he hadn't chosen her.

She leaned her tear-stained face against the cool window pane. Her hot breaths fogged up her view of the passing villages, their red tile rooftops a blood-like blur.

The train finally arrived at the main station in Berlin, and Katja hefted her guitar and bag down the narrow aisle, trying hard not to bang into anyone. It was a difficult feat in the full train, and she got more than one dirty look. She jostled her way through the crowds on the platform until she reached the outdoors. The last time she'd viewed this city, she was with Micah and she'd thought her biggest threat was his colleague, Anna. Well, if Anna was still interested in Micah, she sure had her work cut out for her.

The sky was an angry grey with dark storm clouds billowing in from the east. It fit Katja's mood, but for now she had to push thoughts of Micah out of her head. Sibylle's frightened voice rang in her ears, and she hurried to catch the next city bus that would take her to her neighborhood. The promise of rain arrived with a fury, pelting Katja at sharp angles as she exited the bus at her stop, and she leaned into it. Her damp hand cramped around the handle of her guitar case, and her bag strap bore a heavy groove on her stiff shoulder. By the time she reached the front door of her building, she was soaked and shivering, and her key almost slipped out of her hand.

Exhaustion and cold zapped her strength, but she rallied herself to make it to the second floor.

She accidentally banged the door of their flat with the end of her guitar, but it sounded like a knock, and she heard her sister's voice from the other side. "Who is it?"

"It's me. Katja."

Sibylle turned the lock and opened the door. Katja dropped her things and embraced the frightened girl. She kissed her head. "I'm home now."

Katja closed the door behind her and locked it, though she knew it wasn't enough to keep Horst out. Her mother sat on the sofa, and Katja's heart sunk when she saw her bruised and swollen face.

"Oh, Mama," she whimpered. She sat gently beside her and took her hand. "Everything's going to be okay," she said. "I'll take care of things. I promise."

Katja didn't know where all these brave words were coming from. Her time away had changed her. She was stronger now. She had to be.

She instructed Sibylle, "Get me the phone book, sweetie." Katja looked up the number for a locksmith and dialed. A speedy job to change the lock cost extra, but she had the fruit bowl money and a little more that she'd saved over the last couple months. And this was an emergency.

Afterward, she put the kettle on. A cup of strong coffee would help to both wake her and warm her. A cursory glance around the place told her that her day's work had yet to begin. She walked through each room opening the windows to air out the stale smell. The rain had subsided, but the wind still blew cold, and she made another round to close them again. Then she grabbed a garbage bag from a kitchen drawer and marched into her mother's room. She tossed all of Horst's things into it.

"What are you doing?" Gisela asked, aghast.

"I'm kicking him out."

"You can't do that. He'll…"

"He'll do nothing. I'm calling the police and social services. He's an abuser and it's not safe for Sibylle for him to be here. You're pressing charges."

Fear flashed across her mother's face. "I don't know if I can do that."

"Then I will." Katja looked purposefully into Gisela's tired eyes. "Mama, he attacked me. It's why I left."

Her mother's mouth fell open, but no sound came out.

The kettle whistle blew. "Can you get that, Sibylle?" Katja called out. "It would be great if you could pour it into the bodum carafe."

The young girl seemed relieved to have something to do.

Katja's jaw tightened, and she continued her unpleasant task. She hauled Horst's things into the hall, praying the locksmith would get there before Horst was finished his pub crawl.

She sipped her coffee, but kept moving. She knew if she stopped to rest, her body would revolt and she wouldn't be able to get started again. She counted on the a surge of adrenaline that had kicked in as she started washing the dishes. Her mother watched her and after a few moments, she picked up a tea-towel and began drying. Sibylle pitched in and collected the garbage strewn around the flat, distributing the items in the proper receptacles.

Before too long, the place looked livable. Respectable.

The next thing Katja did was wash all the linens. She attacked the bathroom like her life depended on it. In the other room, she heard the whirl of the vacuum cleaner, and her lips tugged upward. Her mother was alive in that shell somewhere.

The locksmith showed up in the middle of their cleaning spree. She paid him when he finished replacing the handle and double-checked that the door was locked when he left.

There wasn't much in the cupboards, but Katja found enough to cook the three of them a simple pasta dish. It wasn't anything compared to the meals Micah liked to prepare, but he'd taught her a few things, and at least the pasta was properly cooked.

When the sheets were dry, she made the beds and tucked Sibylle in to sleep. Her sister looked up at Katja with wide, blue eyes. "You'll still be here when I wake up?"

Katja stroked her hair, tucking it behind her ears. "Yes. I'll be here. I'm living here now. So don't worry."

"You'll sleep with me again?"

"If you don't mind. Or I could sleep on the sofa."

"No, stay with me. I don't mind."

"Good. Sleep well, *Schatz*. I'll come to bed soon." She kissed the soft skin of the girl's forehead, and closed the door behind her.

Her mother was already in bed. Her medication stripped her of her normal energy, and the beating had exhausted her physically and emotionally. Katja had encouraged her to go, telling her she would take care of Sibylle.

Now she sat on the sofa and waited. She had the police on speed dial. She nodded off, but sprung awake when she heard someone struggle with the door handle. The failed attempt was followed by loud cursing. Katja pushed the button on her phone for the police.

"I'd like to report an incidence of domestic violence."

Katja gave the address and waited. Horst banged on the door, yelling for her mother to open it. Even though she was pretty certain Horst couldn't knock the door open, his temper frightened her and she curled up on the sofa clutching a cushion to her belly.

Sirens sounded outside. Her phone rang. "Yes, you have the right address," she said. "His name is Horst Bergmann. He beat my mother this morning. Six months ago, he attacked me. No, I didn't report it then, but I'm doing it now."

She heard the scuffle in the hallway as the police detained her drunk and aggressive stepfather. The verbal tirade faded as the officers guided him outside, and Katja watched through the window as Horst was moved into the backseat of the green and white cruiser. The neighbors were all out for the show, and she was glad for the witnesses. Horst hadn't made himself any friends here.

She stood at the window until the street was cleared and silence returned to the building. Then she slipped into bed with her sister and fell into a deep sleep.

STRENGTH IN WEAKNESS

MICAH CALLED her several times the next day and left messages. *Call me, please.* Katja ignored them all. He could just go search for another hazel-eyed girl with long honey-blond hair for all she cared.

It wasn't true. The pain that mercilessly squeezed her heart testified to that. She'd had a chance against a dead girl, but Greta was now very much alive and she couldn't compete against that. Everything the locked room stood for and all those years Micah spent chasing Greta was a big part of him. Always would be, even if he wouldn't admit it right now.

Katja woke her mother by gently rubbing her shoulder. "Mama? I'm walking Sibylle to school. When I get back, I'm taking you to the doctor. Get ready while I'm gone, okay?"

Katja held Sibylle's hand as they walked down the tree-lined street. There were shadows under her eyes that were concerning. Sibylle needed to eat better, and to sleep more. And to let go of the burdens that weren't meant for her young shoulders.

Katja hated to bring up the dreaded question, but she had to know. "Sibylle, did your daddy ever… hurt you?"

Sibylle shook her head, and Katja let out a short breath of relief.

"He scares me, though. I'm glad you locked him out."

Katja squeezed her hand. "He scares me, too."

A block from the school, Sibylle gently tugged her hand free. Katja spotted other kids walking, and smiled. Sibylle didn't want to be seen holding her big sister's hand. She understood.

Katja stopped and said, "I think you can make it from here."

"I've been making the whole distance by myself all these years, Katja."

"I know. I just like walking with you." And until she was sure Horst wasn't a danger, she'd keep walking her. "I'll see you after school, okay?"

The late autumn morning chill was lifting, and Katja welcomed the warmth of the sun's rays poking through the remnants of the clouds from yesterday's storm. When she reached her building, she heard someone call her name. She recognized the voice and had wondered how long it would be until she ran into him.

"Hi, Niklas," she said, forcing a small smile. Niklas Reinhardt hadn't changed much. Still thin with a scruffy beard on his chin. He wore work overalls and had grease marks on his arms and hands. A cigarette with a long ash hung out the side of his mouth.

"I heard you were back," he said. He tossed his cigarette and ground it with his boot. "Pulled a good one on your old man."

"Nice to see you, too." She tugged on the door to her building.

"Hey, wait, Katja. We should go out sometime. Like old times." Niklas leaned against his van and flicked his hair back. He smiled crookedly. "Hey?"

Katja couldn't believe she spent two years of her life hanging onto this guy. That she actually let him touch her. She cringed inwardly. "I don't think so."

Niklas huffed and opened his van door. "You go away for six months, and you're a hot shot now?"

"Too hot for you." She went inside and headed upstairs with the sound of Niklas's van roaring to life behind her. She took a deep breath, readying herself for her next task. Surprisingly, her mother was actually ready, dressed in a clean blouse and skirt. The swelling in her face had receded a little, but her skin remained a deep purple.

Katja smiled. "You look good." At least, as good as someone who got beat up the day before could look. "Before we go to the doctor we have to go to the police station. I know you don't want to…"

"I do, Katja." She blinked back tears. "I heard him last night, pounding at the door. I was so afraid he'd get in and kill us all. I can't let that happen. I can't let anything else bad happen to you girls."

Katja took her mother by the arm. "Good. We'll do this together."

They spent much of the morning filling out paperwork. An officer took several pictures of Gisela's face to document the injuries. She looked so vulnerable, standing there, unsmiling as the camera flashed. Katja's heart ached for her mother, sad for her hard life. They were doing the right thing by pressing charges. Things would get better for her family if they stayed strong, she was sure of it.

"We're going to the doctor next," Katja informed the clerk. "I'll have the physician forward her report."

Horst was in jail, and though Katja didn't know how long he'd be detained, they now had a restraining order. Horst wasn't allowed in the building where they lived or anywhere on that block. Katja was determined to make a point of letting all her neighbors know and to get them to promise her they'd call the police if they ever saw him again.

They weren't completely safe, but they were safer.

They stopped at a small market to pick up a few groceries: buns, shaved meat and a block of cheese, a cucumber and a tomato, and they returned to their flat for a light lunch. Gisela was quiet, clearly drained from the morning excursion. Katja's mind kept drifting to Micah despite her efforts to forget about him. She checked her phone and saw he'd called again and left three more text messages. Katja swallowed hard. A part of her wanted to call him back, but their breakup was for the best. She was needed here now. She erased all his messages.

After lunch, Gisela lay down, and Katja decided she had enough time to visit a legal service agency before picking up Sibylle from school.

It was a no-nonsense office on the bottom floor of an old three-story building. Katja told the receptionist why she was there and was in turn told to take a seat. There was a stack of magazines on the end table, but she didn't feel like reading. She checked her phone and stared at the two new messages since lunch. Eventually, he'd give up. He had to see that this was the best thing in the long run. For both of them.

Certainly his mother must be ecstatic. Micah had said she hadn't liked Greta either, but that was where the similarities ended, at least the ones that mattered to people like Frau Sturm. Greta came from a good home. Her family, though not as well off as the Sturms, had money. If Frau Sturm hadn't liked Greta before, she'd probably had a change of heart since meeting Katja.

"Frau Stoltz?"

The lawyer was shorter than Katja, with short grey

hair, a soft belly and a friendly smile. She held out her hand. "I'm Frau Fullermann."

Katja followed Frau Fullermann into her office and sat in the chair opposite the plain, tidy desk. "How can I assist you?" she asked.

Katja relayed her family's situation. "I'm concerned about my sister. I wouldn't want her taken from us because of all of this."

"Horst Bergmann is her biological father?"

"Yes."

"I suspect your sister will be assigned a social worker shortly. If you can prove that you and your mother have the financial means to support her, and that her dwelling place is acceptable and safe, then the social worker will most likely recommend that she remain where she is. Her father may demand to visit her, but we can put in a formal request that visitations occur away from the family home, and in a secure place with the accompaniment of the social worker."

Katja felt sure that with the apartment cleaned up, the dwelling requirements would be met. But finances were another thing. The main reason her mother had put up with Horst all these years was because he'd had a steady job. Now that he was unemployed, that money wasn't coming in anyway. Katja pursed her lips. She had to get a job and quick.

"Thank you, Frau Fullermann. You've given me the information I need."

"Don't hesitate to contact me again should you need my services regarding this matter."

"I will."

Her mind raced as she began her trek to Sibylle's school. The only job experience she had where she could hope for a good reference was from the café in Dresden. It was time to call Renata anyway. She needed to explain her situation and apologize for leaving without saying goodbye. She pulled out her phone and dialed.

Katja arrived at Sibylle's school just as it was letting out. "How was your day?" she asked when her sister appeared.

Sibylle's lips tugged down. "Fine."

"You don't look fine," Katja said as they began the trek back. "Did something happen?"

Sibylle's upper lip quivered, but she remained quiet.

"Sibylle, you can tell me. Were the kids talking about… us?"

She nodded. "They heard about Papa getting hauled away by the police. They weren't too kind about it."

Katja squeezed her shoulders. "Just ignore them. Tomorrow there'll be more exciting bad news for them to gossip about. The thing you have to remember is that you're not your papa. You're you. You make your own choices in life about how you're going to live it. You can't let other people dictate that for you."

Sibylle tilted her head, looking up at Katja's face. "Is that why you came back?"

Katja blinked. "Yes. It is."

She unlocked the door to their flat when they arrived but didn't go in with Sibylle. "I'm going to see Henni," she said. "Lock the door, okay?"

Katja continued up the stairwell to the next floor and tapped on the door of the flat directly above hers. Her stomach swooshed with a new round of nerves. She hadn't seen her friend since she'd left for Dresden months ago, hadn't called or sent any kind of message.

Henni answered the door. She was petite with short, dark hair that had a streak of blue Katja hadn't seen before. She considered Katja coolly. "I heard you were back."

"I'm sorry." Katja nervously clasped her hands near her stomach. "I should've come to visit earlier. A lot's been happening."

Henni waved her inside. "I heard about Horst."

Who hadn't? When you lived in a complex like this one, everyone knew everybody else's business. Bad news sprouted wings, flew along the halls, down the streets to the shops, and through the schools, apparently.

Henni's apartment was laid out exactly the same as Katja's. All the flats were the same, only some were inverted from the others. She took in the familiar room with the same old furniture and wall décor it'd had for the last twenty years Katja had known Henni's family. The lack of change both perturbed her and comforted her.

"How are you?" Katja asked. Henni's teenage brother entered the room, nodded to Katja and turned on the TV.

"Let's go to my room to talk," Henni said.

Henni sat against her large, purple pillow near the wall, and grabbed a tattered stuffed bear that had made a home there since as long as Katja could remember. Katja lay across the foot of the bed and stared up at the string of little white lights Henni had hung over the window.

She pushed out the words she knew she had to say. "I'm sorry for leaving without saying goodbye."

Henni twitched and held the bear tighter. "Yeah, about that."

Katja leaned up on one elbow, facing her friend. "It had to do with Horst."

Henni diverted her eyes. Katja was certain that her memory of finding Horst pinning her down with Katja fighting beneath him was as clear as if she'd witnessed it yesterday.

"And my mother," Katja continued. "She was so out of it with those pills and wouldn't help me. I mean, I thought she wouldn't. Now I know she couldn't help. She wasn't emotionally strong enough." Katja sighed sadly. "It was a spontaneous decision on my part. I thought if I just left, I'd be one less problem for my mother to worry about, and I would be safe from any more unwanted attention from Horst. I didn't mean to leave without telling you. I was in distress, and once I was gone… well it felt too late to look back."

Henni let out a long breath, and her eyes softened. "I knew things were hard for you, Katty. I just didn't know how bad they were."

She tossed her bear to Katja and smiled a little. "So how was your time away? Where'd you go?"

"Dresden." The bear was lumpy with fur missing in patches, but Katja was glad that Henni hadn't thrown it out. She stroked its bumpy head, a move that brought her a nostalgic sort of comfort. "I thought I could break into the music scene there. Make something of myself."

"And?" Henni pushed blue hair off her pixie face. "What happened? Why are you back?"

Katja told her the whole story, not leaving anything out. How Micah picked her up on the street, his obsession with Greta, how one night went from being the happiest day to the worst within moments. She told the story right up to the phone call she received from Sibylle when she stood waiting at the train station.

Henni stared at her with wide eyes and an opened mouth. "You fell in love?"

Katja felt her face contort as she fought to hold back the tears that threatened to well up behind her eyes. "Yeah, I did. But it was stupid, and I'm over it."

Henni moved onto her stomach, legs bent at the knees, feet in the air, her face only centimeters from Katja's. "You don't look over it."

"Well, I'm working on getting over it, so I'm going to stop talking about *him*. The important thing now is that my family needs me, and I have to do everything in my power to keep them safe and provide a stable environment for Sibylle. That's where you come in."

"Me? What do you want me to do?"

"When the time comes, I need you to testify. Tell the judge what you saw that day. How Horst attacked me."

Henni gulped, and Katja knew the idea of speaking out in public, in front of Horst, would be frightening. If he didn't go to jail, Horst could come after her. There was a moment when Katja thought Henni would decline, but then she slowly nodded her head.

"I'll do it. I hate what Horst did to you. I always hear him yelling, and I've been worried about what else he was capable of, that he might pick on Sibylle next. It broke my heart when I heard he'd beat up your mother."

"Thank you," Katja said.

Henni reached for her hand and squeezed. "I'm glad you're back."

"Me, too."

A couple days later, Katja landed a full-time job at a neighborhood bakery and café. The position was in the bakery part, not the café, so instead of serving customers coffee and cake all day like she had at Renata's café, she was in the kitchen washing dishes and scrubbing floors.

Large, rectangular pans encrusted with the edges of almond and crème cake, apple strudel and poppyseed cake, sat in a pile by a commercial-sized stainless steel sink. Katja used a blade to ease the crusts away into the garbage pail and then scrubbed each pan until it was spotless. Herr Bauer was a hard taskmaster, and he didn't balk at raising his voice to tell her when she fell short of his expectations.

He could yell so long as he didn't fire her. She needed this job.

When she was finished with the dishes, she had to scrub the floors. Flour and batter stuck stubbornly to the tile, and Katja had to get down on her hands and knees and scrape with the blade to lift it so she could sweep it off. Then she'd mop it clean, the way it would remain until the baker's shift began the next morning. By the time she was done, her back ached and her hands throbbed.

The job kept her body busy, but her mind was free to roam. Maddeningly, it always took her back to Dresden, back to happier times with Micah. More than once her tears mixed in with the sudsy water in the sink. Today was no different, and she swiped her face angrily. Why couldn't she just forget him!

"Are you okay?"

Katja stiffened at the voice of the boss's son, Matthias. He was around Micah's age, and carried himself in the same manner. Money and privilege. He didn't share Micah's good looks, but he wasn't homely, either. He was about her height with short, blond hair. He had a friendly face and on the few occasions she had seen him, he was always smiling.

She hadn't heard him enter the kitchen where, at this time of day, she normally worked alone. She was mortified. Not only was her face a blotchy mess, but she also felt ugly in her baggy white uniform and apron. Her voice came out in a strangled whisper, "I'm fine."

"When I did this job, I found it helped to listen to music. Just pull your ear buds out when my dad's around."

"You did this job?" Katja couldn't hold in her surprise.

Matthias grinned. "For many years. Believe me, I feel your pain." He grabbed the blade, and bent over to scrape the dough off the floor.

"What are you doing?" Katja asked, bewildered.

He looked up with a smirk. "Helping?"

"You don't…"

"I know, but it'll go faster this way. And…" he added without looking at her, "I wouldn't mind having someone to eat lunch with."

Matthias Bauer wanted to eat lunch with her? Her throat started to seize up, and she squeaked out, "I just broke up with someone."

Matthias handed her the broom, then started filling up the mop bucket. "It's not a date. It's just lunch. I'm hungry."

Of course. Look at her. She was a disaster. How stupid to think that the boss's son was actually interested in her. She kept her head down as she swept, hoping the blush of embarrassment she felt would fade by the time they were done with the floors.

Katja changed back into her jeans and blouse, taking a moment to wash her face and put on a little makeup, thankful she had some old product in her purse. Matthias looked up from his seat in the café and smiled when he saw her. He was just another guy, she told herself. A potential friend. She could really use another friend about now. She sat across from him on a plush, red chair just as two bowls of goulash arrived. The soup was thick with meat and vegetables, with just the right amount of spice.

"This is great," she said after her first taste.

Matthias nodded. "Secret family recipe."

"Really?"

"No." He chuckled. "You can find the same one online."

She patted her smile with a napkin. "So, what kind of music do you like?" she asked since he'd mentioned he listened while working.

Matthias rattled off a list of bands and performers, and Katja was pleased to find he shared her taste in music.

"Do you play?" she asked.

"Play what? You mean an instrument? Nope."

He didn't ask her in return, and she didn't offer the information.

"A lot of great acts come through Berlin, as you probably know," he added. "There's a club around the corner that caters to indies. I'm going this weekend to check it out, if you want to come."

Katja hesitated. "Not a date?"

Matthias cocked a brow. "You just broke up with someone, got that. Also explains why you're crying over the sink. So, no, not a date."

Katja covered her face with her hands. "I'm sorry to assume."

"It's okay. I'm sure guys ask you out all the time. Do you want to go or not?"

"Yes," Katja smiled genuinely for the first time in a long while. "Sounds fun."

AUTUMN IN BERLIN

EVEN THOUGH KATJA worked full-time at the bakery, it wasn't enough to cover the rent, the bills, and the family debt, so the only other answer was for her mother to go back to work.

"I'm doing better," Gisela reassured her. "I feel stronger. It's just such a relief to have him gone."

Katja considered her. She'd taken her mother to get her hair done and bought her some new clothes. Now, with the bruising on her face gone, and a few extra pounds from eating properly, she looked pretty good. "You think you could go back to work? It would only need to be part time."

Gisela nodded. "Maybe I could find something on the weekends."

That would be perfect. Katja worked during the week, so Gisela was home for Sibylle. If she worked on the weekends, Katja could keep an eye on her sister.

With that decided, Gisela spent most mornings looking for work, but her résumé was weak. She didn't get any of the jobs she applied for, and Katja started to worry. Then one day her mother got a call from an employment service. A bank nearby needed janitorial help on the weekends.

"That's perfect," Gisela said. "Funny thing. I don't

even remember applying there, but then again, I applied at so many places. I lost track."

Katja gave her mother a congratulatory hug. Things were going to be okay.

They eased into fall and with Katja and her mother both working, they satisfied the financial requirements of the social worker. Their home was deemed a satisfactory and safe place to raise Sibylle. The trial was over and Horst was now in prison. He wouldn't be out for at least a year, so they had some time to breathe.

It was Friday, and Katja met up with Matthias at the Musique Club again. It had become a weekly ritual, and Katja found she looked forward to it. She entered the dark room, her eyes scanning the faces for Matthias. He grinned when he spotted her and waved her over to his table.

She recognized a few of the faces, other regulars. There was a Berlin equivalent to Sebastian, a rockstar wannabe with an arm draped over a girl, and his sleazy Karl-Heinz-type sidekick. There was even someone like her—the old her—a hopeful singer-songwriter chasing her dreams. She was good, too. But Katja knew that being good wasn't enough to make it. She should talk to the girl, tell her to find something else to do before she had her heart stepped on.

Katja knew the girl wouldn't listen. She'd have to find out her own way.

And who knew, maybe she'd be one of the lucky few who broke out.

Matthias had been really good about giving her space, keeping their relationship platonic. She must've hid her lingering heartache well, because on that night, he draped an arm across the back of her chair. It was innocent enough, just a friendly gesture, but a little while later his hand slipped off the chair and onto her shoulders. She stiffened.

"I'm sorry," Matthias said. He moved his hand back to the chair.

"No, it's okay," Katja said. She missed being touched. His arm around her felt good. Matthias smiled and returned his arm to her shoulder, giving her a little squeeze.

She sipped her beer, making one glass last the whole night. Her wild and crazy days were over. No more getting drunk and making loud judgmental proclamations she regretted the next day. No more letting strange men fawn over her. She had responsibilities now. She couldn't just think about herself anymore.

During a break between acts Matthias spoke into her ear, "Do you want to get out of here?"

Katja flinched. Was he serious? One arm around her back, and he thought she'd be up for making out?

"Katja," Matthias said, "I just mean for a walk, or something. Man, you should see your face."

She giggled with embarrassment. "Sorry, it's just…"

"I know, I know. Guys hit on girls like you all the time."

Katja reached for his hand. "Let's go."

The city lights pushed back at the darkness of nightfall. The odd leaf drifted slowly down to the sidewalk from the nearby linden trees. "You must think I'm so conceited," Katja said.

Matthias shook his head. "Not at all. I'm surprised you're hanging out with someone like me."

Katja stopped to look at him. "What's wrong with you?"

Matthias snorted. "You tell me."

"I did tell you. I just got out of a relationship."

"That was weeks ago. Maybe it's time for you to move on, Katja. Let someone else in."

Maybe Matthias was right. Katja nibbled her lip ring.

He held her gaze. "It drives me crazy when you do that."

She stared back. "Should I stop?"

"No." He leaned in slowly and gently brushed the ring with his lips. Her breath quickened. When she didn't pull away, he placed a hand on the back of her head and kissed her for real.

It was nice. Matthias was a good kisser. Just enough pressure, not too much tongue. Katja tried to relax into it, but all she could think was they weren't Micah's lips. The hand on her head wasn't Micah's hand. The body pressed against hers wasn't Micah's.

She felt numb, and though she didn't push Matthias away or tell him to stop, she grew limp.

Matthias noticed and leaned back. "Whoa." He reached up to wipe a tear off her face. "Was it that bad?"

Katja crumbled and Matthias wrapped his arms around her. She cried into his shoulder, feeling weak and helpless to stop it.

"Too soon," Matthias said, rubbing her back. "I get it." He led her to a bench. "Why don't you tell me what happened?"

Katja pulled tissues out of her purse and blew in a very unattractive manner. "I don't think you want to hear me talk about my problems with another guy."

"Well, not really. But I am curious to know what my competition is. So, spill."

"He asked me to marry him."

"Wow." He leaned his elbows on his knees. "Isn't that a good thing?"

"It lasted *two hours*." She chuckled like she was being

strangled. "I was *engaged* to be married for two hours. How lame is that?"

"You need to give me more, girl. I can't stand it."

Katja blew her nose again, then filled him in on the whole Greta debacle.

"So, you're mad he left you on your engagement night to catch up with his old fling?"

"Yes. Wouldn't you be?"

He huffed. "You're damned right. That guy's an idiot. Not worth another tear, if you ask me."

"To be fair, he had thought she was dead, so it was a big shock for him. And he had loved her once, so of course he'd want to know what happened to her."

"Sure," Matthias conceded. "But did that have to take all night? Especially if the night in question is the one where he'd just asked someone else to spend her life with him?"

"That's my thinking, too. But I still wonder, sometimes, if I'm being too hard on him."

"No, definitely not."

He wasn't exactly unbiased if she could go by the tingling sensation that remained on her lips. She pressed her balled up tissues against her nose and leaned into him. Matthias put his arm around her and said, "I promise I won't kiss you again until you tell me you're good and ready. Okay?"

She sniffled. "Okay."

Katja and her guitar were estranged lovers. In a way she blamed it and her stupid dream for the pain that ballooned in her chest like a fat bear. The instrument, locked in its case, had been propped up in the corner of the bedroom she shared with Sibylle these last few months, and she eyed it from her place on the bed.

It called to her, whispering for her to come back to it. She moseyed over, brought it back to her bed and carefully removed her guitar from its case. She laid it on her knee and caressed the curves of the blond, rosewood frame. Blaming her guitar for her problems was stupid. This instrument had been nothing but a good and faithful friend. It never lied, never betrayed, waited patiently for her to return her affections.

She tuned the strings, noting that they sounded a little dull and she'd need to buy new ones soon. The fingers of her left hand automatically ran up and down the frets, knowing exactly where to land and where to press, while her right hand alternately strummed and picked at individual strings.

She was rusty, for sure, but like riding a bike, playing guitar was something she'd never forget. She played for hours, lost in the world of her favorite folk artists and some of her own songs that belonged to her before the Dresden days. By the end of it the tips of her fingers burned. She knew she'd suffer for a couple days, and she vowed she'd never let her calluses disappear again from lack of use.

Maybe she would perform again. Possibly line up a few gigs around town. Not as a career move, but just for fun. The idea sparked a little life that she needed right now.

She couldn't imagine ever playing "Sun & Moon," or "How Deep Can You Feel" again. "Don't Go Now" remained unfinished and was hidden deep inside a proverbial drawer. She'd have to write new stuff, or she could just stick to cover tunes.

In fact, she'd have to come up with a whole new set list. Her old one reminded her of Micah, and it was just too painful. She needed to move on, and it appeared that he finally agreed. He'd stopped texting weeks ago. Even though it was what she'd wanted and needed, his silence, the fact that he had, in fact, given up on her, crushed her heart.

If only she could stop thinking about him every spare minute of every day, all would be fine. She smirked sadly. She was thankful for one thing. She was glad for Micah's spiritual beliefs, and for the imaginary force field. Breaking up with Micah was the most painful thing she'd ever experienced. It was physically weakening and emotionally crushing. She couldn't imagine what it would've been like for her now if he'd accepted her invitation to join her in his bedroom.

DÉJÀ VU

Katja left early for the Musique Club because she didn't want Matthias to see her lugging in her guitar. It was open mic night, and she signed her name on the form when she walked in. Matthias didn't know about this side of her life, and she wasn't sure if she would go through with it. He'd egg her on if he knew, and she just didn't want the pressure.

Matthias arrived and flashed Katja a smile before taking the seat beside her. They'd stepped back into friendship, and their one and only kiss wasn't mentioned again. Matthias pulled a wool cap off his head and ordered a beer.

"Who's up tonight?" he asked. "Anyone we know?"

Katja held in a smile. "Possibly."

Three acts in, the host of the evening called her name. Matthias slapped the table. "Seriously, Katja? You never thought to mention this?"

"Just shut up and listen, before I change my mind."

Katja eased out and collected her guitar. Her heart thudded when she stood under the spotlight. It'd been a long time since she played in front of a crowd and she was nervous. She closed her eyes and strummed. Her stage fright melted away with the first word she sang. This was her scene. She was made to do this. She belted out Joni Mitchell's "Big Yellow Taxi" like she owned the song. Her voice was strong and powerful, and she felt the rush of knowing the room was hers. Every eye was turned to her, every ear listening.

She finished with a flourish, and the room exploded.

"Hot damn, Katja!" Matthias said, giving her a gigantic hug. "You are a major talent!"

She couldn't stop the huge smile that crossed her face. "It felt good."

Matthias ordered another round of beer. "No, seriously, you're really good."

Katja thanked him again and then forced herself to focus on the next act. At least she tried to. She couldn't stop herself from reliving her performance in her head, basking in the afterglow. She knew for a fact that she'd do it again. She just needed the courage to write a new song.

Matthias walked her home that night. "Are you ready?" he asked, when they got to her building.

She knew what he was asking, and she shook her head. "I'm sorry." Matthias was too good a person to lead on, and until she was really and truly over Micah, she vowed she wouldn't kiss him again. "You shouldn't wait for me," she added. "I fell hard. I don't know when I'm going to be ready to be with someone else."

Matthias's shoulders slumped, but he didn't try to talk her out of it. He sighed, giving her a firm hug and left. Katja didn't know if that meant he'd wait for her or he'd move on. She wasn't sure what she wanted from him, but for his sake, she hoped he'd move on.

Sibylle was asleep when she entered her room. She tiptoed quietly to the bed and kissed her little sister softly on the forehead. She turned on the bedside lamp and Sibylle grunted, but turned over and fell back asleep. Katja picked up her duffle bag and looked inside. Now that she had conquered one fear, she thought maybe it was time to face the others. Her sketchpad and lyric notebook were the only things remaining in the bag. She pulled out the sketch book first, stroked the cover and spine, but didn't open it. She knew what filled the pages. Besides the faces of strangers from the café, and a few of Renata, they were mostly images of Micah Sturm. She pushed the book aside. She wasn't ready for that.

Her lyric notebook wasn't much better. The last song scribbled out was the one she'd written the night everything with her and Micah had imploded. She tossed them both back into the bag and shoved it under the bed. Tomorrow she'd buy a new lyric book.

As time went on, Katja created a name for herself in the indie scene. Like with Maurice at the Blue Note, she was usually offered a full night by the managers of the clubs. She accepted those offers when they came, but she didn't delude herself into thinking they were the gateway to stardom. She sold a few of her old CDs and made extra cash, sure, but it went to buying Sibylle new clothes and boots for the winter, not into a dream fund of any kind. Katja kept her wits about her, keeping her drinking to a minimum. She didn't trust easy flattery, and played to please herself, not worrying if the crowd loved or hated her.

She had a gig that night, where she shared billing with

another indie artist called Simone Pellar. They'd tossed a coin to see who went first and who got the more coveted last spot. Katja won that round, but she still wanted to get there early to show Simone her support.

It grew dark earlier now, and the mid-November frost caused the leaves to fall, leaving skeletal trees in their wake. Katja shivered and ducked her head to the wind. She could've taken a bus or taxi, but that cost money she didn't want to spend. The club wasn't so far away, and in good weather, a pleasant walk.

Her arm grew tired and she shifted her guitar to the other hand. A blast of wind tossed her hair across her face, and she worked to clear it away. Even through her gloves, her fingers burned with the cold. Maybe she should wait at the next bus stop and ride from there.

In her periphery she spotted a silver Audi. Her heart jumped, and then she calmed herself. Lots of people owned silver Audis. But this one didn't pass by. It slowed to a stop. Katja's eyes darted to the driver, and she felt the blood drain from her face. This couldn't be happening. Not again.

The window lowered, and the driver said, "Get in?"

She ducked to make sure her eyes weren't playing tricks on her. "Micah?"

"It's cold," he said. "Let me drive you."

Katja had a very vivid moment of déjà vu. Eight months ago Micah had pulled up beside her on a side street in *Neustadt* and said the same thing. Getting in his car that night had changed her life. (Probably saved it, but that was beside the point.)

She couldn't take her eyes off his face. She was mesmerized by his eyes, his bone structure, the lips she fantasized over every night in her dreams. She sincerely never thought she'd ever see him again in the flesh.

"Katja? Please, I'll take you to your gig."

Her breath hitched. "How do you know where I'm going?"

He nodded to the guitar in her hands. "Good guess? Get in. You're freezing to death."

As if of their own accord, her legs moved around the front of the car, and she found herself placing her guitar in the back seat. Micah reached over and opened the passenger door, and she got in, feeling strangely detached. None of her senses could be trusted right now. Her emotions were in a turmoil and her body responses completely out of control. Her heart rate soared and a cold sweat broke out on the back of her neck. She sat centimeters away from the man who'd torn her heart in two and her world to shreds. Did he not understand how hard she had to work to move on? In one second flat, she was back to where she was in the beginning. Completely destroyed.

She hated him for the power that he held over her. And she loved him. She wanted to rip his eyes out with her nails, while at the same time she wished she could kiss him hard on the lips.

She opted for clasping her hands on her lap and staring hard at her wet shoes.

SHADOWS PATTERN ON THE ROAD

He signaled and steered the Audi back into traffic. When he didn't say anything, Katja finally asked, "Where are we going?"

Micah's gaze darted to Katja and then back to the road. "My place."

She couldn't hide the surprise in her voice. "You have a place in Berlin?" She added smugly before he could answer, "Daddy got you another job?"

His jaw tightened. "Yup."

She squirmed at the thought of being alone with Micah in another one of his apartments. "I can't. I have a gig in an hour."

"Simone Pellar is opening, so you actually have two hours."

Katja turned sharply. "Are you stalking me?"

He smirked. "Define stalking."

"You know what I mean." She folded her arms in defiance. "Why would I want to go with you to your place?"

"Because it's warmer. And I'd hoped we could talk."

She grunted and looked away. "I have nothing to say."

"Well, I do. Katja. I just can't leave things the way we parted. All I'm asking is that you give me a chance to explain. Then if you want me to go, to leave you alone forever, I will."

She rolled her eyes like it didn't matter to her one way or the other, but in actual fact she was dying to hear what he had to say. Not knowing what had happened between Micah and Greta was like a worm in her mind, constantly wiggling through the mire and mud of her imagination.

They arrived at a modern, upscale apartment building and Micah tapped in a code on a number pad to enter the underground parking place.

Katja left her guitar in the car, knowing she was too far from her gig to walk now, and like it or not, Micah would have to drive her. "It's safe here, I gather," she said, noting the security cameras in the corner. Micah nodded.

They entered the elevator and Micah pushed the number ten.

"Wow, tenth floor. The very top. You must have a stunning view." She was babbling. She didn't care about the floor or the view. She just felt overwhelmed by the fact that Micah Sturm stood so near her, shoulder to shoulder, facing the door.

"Yes," he mumbled, "it's nice."

It was more than nice. Katja fought to keep her expression blank when she entered and scouted it out, but she was astounded. The apartment was impeccably furnished with all the latest in interior design, with high glass windows overlooking the heart of Berlin. It made the flat she shared with her mother and sister feel once again like a hovel, when ten minutes ago, she was quite proud of what she'd done to make it livable and homey.

"We're here," she snapped. "Say what you have to say."

"Can I get you a drink?"

"I doubt you have anything strong enough to satisfy me at the moment."

Micah opened a cupboard and removed a bottle of her favorite red wine. He fished out a corkscrew from one of the drawers, opened it and poured her a glass. At her look, he explained, "I'd hoped to bring you here one day."

He handed it to her, and she worked to keep her hand from quivering as she accepted it. She took a long drink and sat in the nearest chair in the living room. She set the glass down on the table beside her, afraid she might spill. She didn't need to add to her list of embarrassments.

"So, talk."

Micah pulled a matching chair closer, until he sat directly in front of her. He propped his elbows on his knees, which were nearly brushing hers, and tented his fingers. Her core temperature skyrocketed when he locked eyes with her. She felt captured, imprisoned. She wanted to flee, but felt helplessly trapped.

"I want to be completely honest with you," he said, "so some of this will be hard for me to say, and for you to hear."

Her hands gripped the armrests of her chair as if she were about to take off in a speeding jet plane. She'd never flown anywhere, but she guessed it felt like this: pulse rushing, palms sweating, senses screaming that the elevator floor had dropped out from beneath you.

Micah swallowed, then began, his words pouring out like paint onto the floor. "It's true that in the beginning of our relationship, yours and mine, I was looking for a way to resolve myself of my sins. Consciously or subconsciously, I'm not sure, but it doesn't matter. I wanted, needed, to atone for losing Greta. I believed she was dead and that it was my fault.

"When I saw her standing there that night, alive, it was

like I'd grabbed onto an electric fence and couldn't let go. She was *alive*. You don't know what that did to me, to find out once and for all that I wasn't responsible for another person's death.

"That should've been enough for me. I should've left her standing there and followed you into our flat. You don't know how many times I've whipped myself for that.

"But Greta had this miserable hold on me for years. She's manipulative and cunning and I was a sucker to her charms."

Katja choked out. "Did they work on you again?"

Micah hesitated. "I could lie and say no, but her tentacles had me bound for a very long time. Even though I knew I should've left her immediately, I couldn't stop myself from following her. I knew I was risking losing you, but I naively thought that you would forgive me. I just had to hear her out."

He paused to run fingers through his curls, and took in a long breath.

"It wasn't enough for her to find me. Even though she didn't want me, she didn't want to share me. I thought the timing of her arrival to be very coincidental. She eventually revealed to me that she'd been in contact with my mother. She *knew* I was going to ask you to marry me that night.

"I should've known by the way she looked at you that her goal was to break us up. She was stronger than me. For that I'll never forgive myself.

"By the time she finished the convoluted tale of her selfish pursuit of self-discovery in the Swiss Alps, the sun was rising. I knew I'd blown it. Any sliver of affection I'd ever had for her had been ground to dust in the hours it had taken for her to recite her misadventures, and it had blown away into the Elbe.

"The only girl I could think of at that moment was you. You've been the only girl on my heart and mind, day and night, since. I'm still chasing a girl, Katja, but this time it's you. It will always be you."

Katja blinked hard, her mind racing to comprehend. "She's been in Switzerland all this time, and never bothered to tell anyone?"

"She impulsively traveled there the night I passed out. She needed to 'clear her head.' Then, when she realized there was a manhunt for her, I guess it made her feel special and important. That was when she decided she'd let the legend grow."

Katja was astounded. "She didn't care what it was doing to you?"

Micah sighed. "Apparently not. She'd grown tired of me, and didn't think I'd let her go without a fight. She was probably right about that. Eventually, she did contact her mother, but made her promise not to tell anyone."

"Why did she contact your mother?"

"Her mother and my mother are friends. When I told my mother I was planning to ask you to marry me, she in turn told Greta's mother, who told Greta."

The whole story was just so warped and crazy. Katja rubbed her temples. She had to keep her wits about her, but she felt her defenses slipping. "How long have you been living in Berlin?"

"Two months."

"Why didn't you contact me earlier? You know where I live."

"I didn't think you were ready to see me."

She worked the ring in her lip. "Why do you think I'm ready now?"

"You've started playing your guitar again."

Oh, Lord. Micah really did know her.

"I assumed it would be tough for you here," Micah said, leaning back. "It had to be. I wanted to help you, but I knew you wouldn't accept cash. You're stubborn that way."

She huffed. "I'm not stubborn."

"Believe me," he said without smiling. "If there's one thing you are, Katja, it's stubborn. At least I was able to help your mother."

"*You* got Mama that job?"

"She's proven to be an excellent worker."

Katja shook her head. Why was she not surprised? "So, if I move to Frankfurt, are you going to move there, too?"

Micah's eyes darkened. "No. As I told you when I picked you up tonight, if you want me to go away, I will."

Katja's heart stammered, and her mouth grew dry. Her mind and emotions were like a ball rolling out of control down a hill.

"I'm going to be late for my gig," she said quietly.

Micah gathered his keys. "I'll take you."

SING ME ONE MORE SONG

KATJA COULD BARELY THINK STRAIGHT. Her heart hammered in her chest during the whole ride to the club, and she couldn't come up with one word to say to Micah. She'd spent every waking moment, and most of her sleeping ones, working hard to forget Micah. Not to forgive him. And yet, here he was asking her to do just that.

Micah parked and reached for Katja's guitar before she could retrieve it. "I'll carry it for you."

She remembered all the other times Micah had carried her guitar for her, how he proudly proclaimed himself to be her groupie, and her heart softened a little.

"Are you coming in?" she asked when they reached the door.

"I'd like that," he said, "a lot."

They entered the darkened room in time to catch the last song of Simone's set. The stage lights had a blue lens that cast a cool hue into the audience, making everyone's face look whiter than normal. Matthias was there, and he rushed to her side when the song ended. "Where were you?" His ghostly expression chastised her. "I thought you said you'd be here for Simone."

"I meant to. I just… ran into someone."

Matthias's gaze moved to Micah and to Katja's guitar

case in his hand. His eyes narrowed. "That's not the jerk who dumped you on your engagement night for his old girlfriend, is it?"

"Matthias!"

Micah held out his hand. "It is, actually. I'm Micah."

Matthias's face twisted in disbelief. "Excuse me if I don't shake your hand."

Katja groaned.

Matthias wasn't finished. "Do you want me to show him out?"

Did she? Matthias and Micah bore down on each other like two cocks wanting the same hen. Only one of them had claimed her heart. Only one of them still did.

"No." She sighed. "He can stay."

Matthias shrugged on his jacket. "Fine."

"I'm sorry," she said.

"It's okay." He stuck his fists in his pockets. "It's your call."

Katja watched him as he headed for the door. He was stopped by friends before he had a chance to leave, and she hoped he'd change his mind and stay for her set.

"I like him," Micah said with a grin.

"I don't think he likes you."

"He cares about you. We have that in common."

The host motioned for Katja to get ready. When Katja had left her apartment that evening, she never in a million years imagined that the night would've gone like this. That Micah would be sitting in the room, and not at the back this time, but at a table front and center, watching her play.

She spoke with the manager of the bar and the guy who helped with the sound. She reviewed her set list. A song was missing. She knew how to end it now. Quickly, she took her new lyric notebook from her bag. She remembered the words of the song by heart, but quickly scribbled out the lyrics to the third verse. She smiled. It was finished now.

She waited for her introduction, then entered the spotlight on the small stage. She never felt alone when she had her guitar nuzzled against her belly. They were a team, and they could conquer any giant together. Including this one.

"Thank you," she said as the welcoming applause faded. She ran through her set, sticking with covers and a few new songs that didn't have anything to do with love, and telling humorous stories in between. She was good at what she did, and she quickly had the crowd engaged and listening to her every word.

Her hour blew by quickly, as most of her performances did for her. "I'm going to end my set with a song I started several months back and just finished ten minutes before I got on stage tonight. It's dedicated to the one who broke my heart."

Micah's dark eyes drilled into her, his mouth in a firm line. She broke the gaze, snapping her eyes shut, knowing this was going to hurt.

Don't go now
I know it's late and the light is growing dim
But I just like the way
You feel beside me on the front steps, not yet
Sing me one more song,
The one about the girl, who finds the whole wide world

She risked a peek. Micah looked stricken by her words. She had to look away.

Don't go now
I know it's late and the dark is folding in
But I just like the way
Your fingers close around my hand, so grand
And sing me one more song
The one about the girl who finds the whole wide world

So far she had managed to sing without her emotions threatening to crack her voice, but now, as she prepared to enter the last verse, she had to squeeze her eyes shut and focus on staying strong.

Don't go now
I know it's late and the light is spreading thin
But I just like the way
The shadows pattern on the road, don't go
And sing me one more song,
The one about the boy who never let her go

The crowd roared, and the room began to spin. She thanked the crowd, keeping her eyes focused on the back of the room. She packed up her guitar, her heart pounding against her chest. She knew Micah was watching her, but she couldn't face him. She couldn't bear the look of grief on his face.

He didn't give her a choice.

"Katja?"

"I wrote it while waiting for you. Call it our engagement song."

He reached for her arm. "I didn't mean to hurt you."

She sighed. "But you did. I want to forgive you, Micah, and I do, but… I just need more time."

"You can have as much as you want."

She didn't know what she was promising him, if anything. "I have to go." She left Micah standing near the stage, and was surprised to see Matthias waiting by the door.

"I thought you left," she said to him.

"Nah. I had to see you play." He cocked an eyebrow. "I hate to say it, but that last song rocked."

She shook her head sadly. "I don't know if I'll ever sing it again."

For the first time, Matthias carried her guitar case for her. "You look beat. I'll take you home."

"Thanks." She couldn't stop herself from taking a peek over her shoulder at Micah. He stared at her looking bereft. In her heart, she knew she was leaving with the wrong guy, but she couldn't help herself. She wanted Micah to know what it felt like.

LOST & FOUND

The next day was Sunday, her day off, and Katja slept in. The timing was good, because she didn't have the physical or emotional energy to get out of bed. As she lay there in the dim winter morning light, the events of the night before replayed in her mind, over and over again. Micah's return into her life was an unexpected wrench. She needed some downtime to process it.

Plus, she didn't want to risk running into Matthias again. She liked him as a friend only, and she felt badly that she'd let him believe there was a chance for something else. Next time she saw him, she'd have to tell him how she felt. She hoped their friendship would survive. Her heart couldn't bear losing another person she cared about so dearly.

Her cell phone rang on the side of her bed, and she groaned. She wasn't up to speaking to anyone, especially Micah or Matthias. She picked it up, expecting to see one of their names on the screen, but instead it was her lawyer's name, Tanya Fullermann.

"Katja Stoltz," Katja answered.

"Hello, Katja. It's Tanya Fullermann. I have news you may not be happy to hear."

Katja's heart skipped. "What is it?"

"Horst has been released on probation."

Blackness closed in on the edges of Katja's eyes, and she pinched them tight. "Oh."

"Your restraining order against him is still in effect, but I wanted to make sure you knew he was back on the streets."

Katja sprung out of bed, whisking to the front door to make sure it was locked. Sibylle was watching television while eating breakfast. A startled look crossed her face. "What's wrong?"

"Uh, nothing, just checking the door."

She heard Gisela banging around in the kitchen, and she slipped in to tell her the news, keeping her voice low.

Gisela's hand reached for her throat. "What are we going to do?"

"There's nothing we can do, except use extra caution. We can't let Sibylle out alone."

Gisela nodded, but Katja knew she was concerned. Sibylle would turn twelve soon. They couldn't keep her under lock and key forever. She had a life. Or at least, she should have a life. She needed friends and hobbies that took her beyond home and school. She wouldn't put up with Katja escorting her everywhere for much longer.

She shared her concerns with Henni later that day when she dropped by for a visit.

"I'll help watch her," she said. Her hair streaks were pink now. "Sorry I missed your show last night," she added. "How did it go? I heard Simone Pellar was really good."

"You heard how Simone's set went, but not mine?"

"Well, actually, I heard yours was amazing and that you did some crazy powerful song at the end, but I wanted to hear it from you."

"Micah showed up last night."

"*The* Micah?"

Katja nodded.

"And?" Henni poked her in the ribs. "Come on. Spill!"

"And, I sang the song I wrote the night he left me. To hurt him. Then I left with Matthias. To hurt him. I'm an awful person."

"Oh, Katja." Henni pulled her into a hug. "The fact that you feel awful about what you did just proves you're not an awful person. Besides, he deserved it."

Katja pulled free and pressed fingers against her eyes. She was so tired of tears. "Yeah, he did, but now it's over, and I don't feel any better."

"It takes time," Henni said with a knowing look. "It just takes time."

Katja threw all her pent-up energy into work the next day. The physical act of viciously scrubbing dishes didn't calm her raging emotions at all. Micah was here in Berlin, messing with her mind. If she didn't have her mother and sister to worry about she'd just catch the next train to wherever. But she did have them. She was stuck. What was she doing with her life? How long would she be washing dishes and scrubbing floors?

She examined her hands. Red and chapped, they looked like they belonged to an old lady. She'd taken to chewing her nails lately to relieve stress. Thick calluses had formed on the tips of her fingers again from playing guitar.

At least the dishes were done. She just needed to do the floor and then she could go. Hopefully, she'd be gone before Matthias showed up. She just didn't have the energy to deal with him right now.

She grabbed the blade and got down on her hands and knees to scrape the floor. She was halfway done when she heard a male voice call her name.

It wasn't Matthias's voice. She froze on the spot. No, please. She didn't want him to see her like this: sweaty and grimy, dressed in scrubs, on her hands and knees.

"Katja?" he called again.

She turned, and Micah was standing in the doorway, looking like a model, wearing clean, name brand jeans and a crisp shirt. A shocked expression crossed his gorgeous, clean-shaven face.

She couldn't feel more humiliated. "What are you doing here?" she mustered

"I thought I'd drop in for coffee."

She flung her hand. "You missed the café by about two meters. It's behind you."

"I know. I thought you worked there."

"No, I work in the bakery, back here." She wished the floor she'd been scraping would just open up and swallow her.

"When does your shift end?" he asked. "Should I wait for you?"

Oh, God, no. "I really should go home. I need to shower…"

Her phone buzzed in her pocket. Now what? She dug it out and answered it. Her face blanched as she listened to her mother's frantic voice. She sprung to her feet. "I'll be right there, Mama."

"Is something wrong?" Micah asked

"Sibylle is missing. Horst is out on bail, and my mother thinks she's with him."

"Isn't she in school?"

"It's a school holiday. I have to go home."

"Of course. I'll drive you."

She didn't want to go anywhere with him, especially looking like she did, but he would get her home faster than walking or transit.

"Okay." She told Herr Bauer she had a family emergency and had to leave before the floors were done. He bellowed his disapproval, and she wondered if she'd still have a job the next day.

She didn't speak during the trip over, sitting as close to the passenger door as possible. She hated how the bakery made her smell and didn't want Micah to sniff her. And she couldn't believe she could care about something so vain when her sister was missing. She tapped her fingers restlessly on the arm rest, just wanting to be home *now*.

Micah hooked his blue tooth around his ear. Katja didn't see how he connected to the person on the other end, but she perked up when he started talking.

"His name is Horst Bergmann. Out on parole. I need to verify his whereabouts. I'm with the older daughter now. The younger one is missing and they are concerned she's with Bergmann without authorization."

A pause. "Yes, that's fine."

"Who were you talking to?"

"My lawyer. He's putting a call into the parole board. They'll locate your step-father."

The lawyer hadn't called back by the time they arrived at the building. Katja raced up the stairs with Micah right behind her. She banged on the door.

"Mama, it's me!"

Gisela opened the door, her eyes puffy and red. "I'm sorry Katja. I fell asleep. When I woke up she was gone."

"She could be anywhere," Micah said. "You can't know for sure she's with Horst."

Gisela squinted. "Who is this, Katja?"

"Oh, Mama, it's Micah. You've met before, a long time ago."

Gisela nodded slowly. "That Micah."

Yes, *that* Micah.

Katja raced to her room. Just in case. Her sister may have returned without her mother noticing. "Sibylle?"

The bed was neatly made. There was no sign of her sister. Katja took a moment to quickly change her clothes to a clean shirt and jeans. She put her winter coat back on.

"I'm going to search for her," she announced. "Mama, stay here in case she comes back. Call me the minute she does. I'll let you know if I find her."

Katja skipped down the steps with Micah on her heels. When they got to the street, Katja didn't know which way to turn. Left or right. She chose right, the direction of the school. But why would she go there? She spun and went the opposite direction. What did it matter where Sibylle would choose to go? If Horst had her, she wouldn't be anywhere near here.

Micah clasped her arm. "Katja?"

"I don't know what to do." Katja ran her rough fingers through her ponytail. "I feel so helpless. If he does anything to her. If he hurts her…"

She buried her face in her hands and instantly felt Micah's strong arms encase her. She shivered in his embrace.

"Shh," he said, stroking her hair. "We'll find her."

Katja pulled herself free. She had to get a hold of

herself. She wasn't going to find Sibylle by weeping on Micah's shoulder.

Micah stuffed his hand in his pocket and pulled out his phone. "Sturm." He nodded and said, "Thanks."

Katja stared at him waiting.

"They've located Horst. He doesn't have her."

When Micah said those words it was like he'd lifted a bag of rocks off her back. She let out a hard breath of relief. But her sister was still missing. "Where is she then?"

"Let's keep looking."

They started walking, and Micah asked, "Have you contacted her friends? Maybe she's gone to one of their homes?"

Katja let out a soft groan. "She doesn't have any friends. She should have, but she's… afraid, and since I've been back, I think I've instilled even more fear, not less. She should have friends. Our lives are so messed up."

This time it was Katja's phone ringing. "Mama?"

"She's here, Katja. She's safe."

"Oh, thank God. Where was she?... Henni's? What was she doing there? No wait. I'll be home shortly."

She looked at Micah, and her eyes glistened. Tears of gladness. "She's safe."

"That's good," he said. "That's really good."

"Yes, it is. And now I have to go home and kill my friend."

When they got back, Katja rushed to Sibylle and squeezed her tight. "You scared me."

"I'm sorry, Katja," she whimpered. "I was just watching TV with Henni."

Katja glared at her neighbor. "How could you?"

"What? I just came to talk to you and found Sibylle watching TV alone, *again*. I felt sorry for her. I didn't think it was a big deal."

"You could've left a note or sent me a text or something."

"I figured Sibylle would be back here before you or your mother got home. I didn't know Gisela was sleeping."

Katja heard the word Henni left off this time. *Again.*

Katja guided Sibylle to the sofa and sat down with her. "Next time, just tell me."

"Geez, we didn't even leave the building." Henni took in Micah, her gaze running up and down his body and landing back on his eyes. She smiled and extended a hand. "I'm Henni, Katja's lousy friend and neighbor."

"Micah. Pleased to meet you."

Henni's mouth formed a small circle.

Micah grinned. "Yes, *that* Micah."

"Well, if you all don't need me anymore," Henni said, heading for the door, "I think I'll make myself scarce. Bye."

Now that the emergency was over, Katja didn't know what to do. Micah stood with his hands clasped. She sat pressed next to Sibylle with her arms circled around her.

Gisela sat in the chair opposite watching them. She stood and approached Micah, and Katja wondered what she'd say. Would she chase him out now?

Instead, she surprised her with this: "Thanks so much for your help today, Micah. Would you like to stay for *Mittage Essen*?"

Katja's jaw dropped. Her mother invited him to lunch? She had to be kidding.

THE BOY WHO
NEVER LET HER GO

THE MOMENT FELT surreal with the four of them, Katja with her mother and sister, and Micah Sturm, sitting around their small kitchen table in dim lighting, eating veal cutlets and potato salad.

The veal was overcooked and the potatoes not cooked enough. Micah was every bit a gentleman, complimenting Gisela on her cooking, but Katja knew that Micah would blow them both out of the water with his own version of the same meal.

It was her day to be mortified and humiliated in every way possible, it seemed.

"Katja tells me you're in banking," Gisela said. "From a family of bankers."

"This is true. It's not the most exciting work, but I'm grateful for it."

Gisela just hummed.

"So, Katja." Micah placed his fork down and looked at her. "There was a reason I stopped by the café earlier. I have something I want to tell you."

Katja nibbled her lip ring. Apparently finding her scrubbing floors like a common maid—worse actually, Micah hired maids, and they never had to get on their hands and knees—hadn't dissuaded him. He could've bolted a long time ago, and yet he remained. She nodded for him to continue.

"I'm friends with a movie producer in town, and I gave him your CD. He makes independent films and is always looking for soundtrack music."

Katja's throat suddenly went dry. She took a long drink from her glass of water. "Um, that's an old CD now."

"I told him that. He listened anyway and really liked it. Wants to know if you have anything new he can hear."

Katja shook her head. She had new material, but there was no way she could afford to record again.

Micah steadied his gaze on hers. "I know what you're thinking."

"Ha," she scoffed. "You read minds now,too?"

"I think I can read your mind."

"Really?"

"I want to underwrite your next CD. Consider it an investment."

"A high-risk investment."

"I like to take risks."

"Since when?"

"Since I met you."

Katja lifted her fork to her mouth and chewed the tough meat, taking her time to swallow. Micah was full of surprises.

Gisela rubbed Katja's arm. "It sounds like a good opportunity."

Katja pushed back from the table. "Would you excuse us?" She motioned for Micah to follow her out into the hall. The aroma of their meal followed them and mingled with the smells emanating from the other flats.

She hooked her fingers into her belt loops. "Why are you doing this?"

"I want to show you that I get it now, why you need to do your art. It's who you are."

Did he really? Or was he just saying what he thought she wanted to hear. "But I've already given it up."

"If that were true, you wouldn't still be gigging."

Katja folded her arms and glanced away. If she did this, she would be tied to Micah for a long time. She didn't know if she could survive that.

"You're really good, Katja, and I want to help you. I've already booked studio time."

Her head snapped up. "I have a job, you know. I can't just leave whenever."

"I spoke to Matthias, and he told me your hours so I could book around them."

"You spoke to Matthias?"

"Yeah. He's cool. He's glad you have this chance to record."

"Even though it means I'll be spending time with you?" she asked incredulously. He really must've moved on.

"I told him I'd do anything to help you, to make you happy. He wants the same thing."

Katja pressed her fingertips to her forehead. How did her life get so completely out of control?

"Okay, I'll do it. But not because you want me to, or because Matthias wants me to, but because I want to."

"Great. The first session is in three days."

"Fine. Text me the address, and I'll meet you there." She paused at the door before entering. "And don't try to call me in the meantime." She left him standing in the hall, and rushed passed the startled faces of her mother and sister to her room.

Katja spent the next three days stewing. Whether she was at work, or at home, or lying awake at night in her bed, she couldn't get Micah off her mind.

Why did he have to show up? She had everything under control. She'd given up her dreams, and had accepted her role as caregiver to her mother and sister. Their needs came first and she was willing to wash dishes and scrub floors if that was what it took. She might have gone back to school someday, became a secretary or something. She was happy enough to play her guitar just for fun. She liked hanging out with Matthias, and maybe one day she would've had room in her heart to be more than just friends with him.

Damn Micah Sturm! He'd ruined everything.

Now her heart wanted things she knew were bound to disappoint and hurt her. It wasn't too late for her to change her mind. Micah promised he would go if she asked him to.

She decided then, as she tossed and turned the night before her first studio session, that was what she'd do. She'd cancel her sessions, tell Micah to leave and pick up the pieces that remained of her heart and keep going.

Katja groaned at her image in the mirror the next morning. The bags beneath her eyes betrayed her. She did her best to make herself presentable, choosing her best jeans, a fine-knit sweater and a pair of fashionable winter boots she'd recently splurged on. A little makeup went a long way. She brushed her hair out, deciding to leave it loose, and even put on a pair of hoop earrings.

She didn't know why she cared about how she looked if she was just going to say goodbye, but the memory of her in her bakery uniform and her disheveled appearance from the last time Micah saw her burned in her mind. She still had some pride.

She hugged her mother and kissed Sibylle's forehead on her way out.

"Have fun," Gisela said. Katja didn't have the heart to tell her she wasn't going through with it.

The studio was on the edge of a residential area at the back of a brick building. If she hadn't had the address, she'd never have known it was there. It made her think it couldn't be much of a studio.

Micah crossed the room when he saw her arrive, his face washed with relief like he thought she might not come. "Hey," he said. "Come have a look around." He didn't waste time on pleasantries, like he knew he had to get his words in quickly before she could say hers.

The studio was more impressive on the inside. The walls had folded molding, like a large deck of cards tented on its side, that deadened the sound. The soundboard and instruments all looked top notch. A glass partition separated the sound engineer from the vocal microphone. There was a separate room for the drums.

"This is Felix," Micah said, pointing to the guy in the engineer's chair. "He's your producer."

Felix stood, tall and lanky, with long hair pulled back into a low pony tail. He reached for her hand. "So good to meet you. I've heard your stuff. I can't wait to get started."

Katja frowned. Micah was smooth. "Actually," she started, "I wasn't..."

Micah grabbed both of her shoulders, ducking low, forcing her to look at him. "You're here now. You might as well record one track."

It was like he knew she was going to bail. "How…"

"You arrived without your guitar."

The guy was just so attentive to her. How could she say no? "One song."

Micah guided her into the vocal booth and closed the door behind him. She mentally reviewed her repertoire. It was hard to choose. All her best songs were about Micah. She placed her hands on her hips and admitted, "I don't know which one to do."

"Do the one you sang the other night," Micah said.

Katja glanced at him, surprised. "You know I sang that song because I thought it would hurt you."

"It did hurt me, but it also encouraged me."

She was stunned. "How so?"

"It's called, 'Don't Go.'"

Katja slumped onto the studio sofa. Micah sat tentatively beside her. "Are you all right?"

"I don't get you," she said. "You could have any girl. There are a lot of pretty, intelligent girls in your…" She waved a hand, "… class. They don't have the baggage I carry."

"I don't want those girls. Katja, listen to me. Besides being immensely attractive, you are a good, decent person. I know you don't believe that about yourself, but it's true. You're selfless and kind. You make me want to be a better person. You taught me to hope.

"None of those girls come close to what you are to me. Especially a certain one I refuse to name."

He reached for her hand, and she let him take it. "I love you. I've never stopped."

A lump had grown in Katja's throat, and she found it hard to swallow.

"Please," Micah pleaded. "Say something."

"I really want to kiss you."

Micah huffed, his face bright with relief. "I think that's a fantastic idea."

His lips touched hers, first cautiously and tenderly, and then urgently. She responded in kind, like she hadn't had anything to drink in days and Micah was a cold glass of water. His lips played with her lip ring.

"Do you like it?" she asked between kisses. "You've never said."

"Yes, I *like* it." His mouth ran along her jawbone, down her neck, and she shuddered under his touch.

"I love you, Micah Sturm."

He paused, and then his lips trailed back to hers. "You don't know how desperate I've been to hear you say those words."

"Then I better say them again. I love you."

Micah slipped to the floor, kneeling, and Katja wondered what he was doing. He reached into his pocket. "I've been carrying this around since the day you left, hoping I'd have another chance to give it to you."

Her pulse took off. Was he...?

He held a dainty item between his forefinger and thumb. It glittered in the studio lights. Her engagement ring. "Katja, may I place this back on your finger?"

She gasped, then held out a shaky hand. "Yes."

Micah slipped it on, then he let out a hoot and swooped Katja up in his arms. He called out to Felix who'd been spying on them from the other side of the glass. "We need to rebook!"

Felix laughed and waved them off.

Katja giggled as Micah carried her out of the studio and to his car. She didn't know where he was taking her and she didn't care, so long as they were together. Finally, and forever.

EVER AFTER

Micah and Katja were married in the oldest church in Berlin on a snowy day in February. It was a small ceremony celebrated with family, a few of their Berliner friends and a handful from Dresden. Renata and Maurice came, of course, and Sebastian and Yvonne even attended. Sebastian said he had a gig in Berlin with his band anyway.

The two steeples of the ancient Nikolaikirche had been sheathed in snow, looking like two angels standing guard. Though a large part of the structure had been destroyed in the war and subsequently rebuilt and reopened as a museum, the foundation went back 800 years. The building represented the old and the new.

Frau Sturm accepted her defeat in the matter of her son's choice of bride, and after a couple of drinks at the reception, managed to welcome Katja into the family.

Katja moved into Micah's tenth-floor flat as Frau Micah Sturm, stunned to discover that the entire building was, in fact, owned by Micah's father. As a result, her mother and sister were invited to live in one of the smaller ground-floor suites at a greatly reduced rent. Her mother was ecstatic. Not only was the flat clean and beautiful and in a good neighborhood, it was secure, a feature that meant a lot, knowing that her soon to be ex-husband wandered about freely. Sibylle changed schools to one closer to their new home, and she flourished in her studies.

Katja couldn't be happier. She spent her days writing music and sketching, and her evenings with her new husband making love.

She continued to perform as the years went on, becoming a national name in the indie music scene. The country knew her as award-winning singer-songwriter, Katja Stoltz-Sturm.

But the only names she cared about were the ones she held at home. *Daughter, sister* and *wife*. Katja snuggled in under Micah's arm as he ran through the channels on the TV and rubbed her rounded belly. And this new name: *Mama*.

the end

If you enjoyed reading *Sing Me a Love Song*, please help others enjoy it too.

Lend it: This ebook is lending-enabled, so please share with a friend.

Recommend it: Help others find the book by recommending it to friends, readers' groups, discussion boards and by suggesting it to your local library.

Review it: Please tell other readers why you liked this book by reviewing it at Amazon.

Want more LIGHT & LOVE Sweet Romance?

YOUR LOVE IS SWEET
book 2 in A Light & Love Sweet Romance

Singer songwriter Eva Baumann has a celebrity crush on Sebastian Weiss. He's perfect to love because there was no way they could ever be a thing. She's a nobody. He's a heartthrob. Hiding an infatuation is easy for her because, since her accident, hiding is what she did best.

Sebastian Weiss's band climbed the charts, seemingly overnight, and he's finally living the dream.All he has to do is write enough songs to produce a second album. The bad news is he hasn't written a new song in over a year.

Sebastian stumbles into the Blue Note Pub in time to hear Eva Baumann perform a hauntingly beautiful song. Could this girl be the answer to defeating his writer's block?

Eva and Sebastian begin a complicated writing relationship that leads to more. But Sebastian has a secret that will devastate them both. Can Eva forgive? Or will she miss out on Sweet Love?

Read on for the first chapter of YOUR LOVE IS SWEET!

∼

MEET GINGER GOLD

If you like your sweet romance mixed with a light-hearted mystery, I invite you to give my new cozy mystery series a try.

The Ginger Gold Mystery series is a fun, 1920s era romp featuring thirty-year-old fashionista war widow Ginger Gold.

To make sure you don't miss the next new release, be sure to sign up for Lee's readers' list and get 4 FREE short stories!

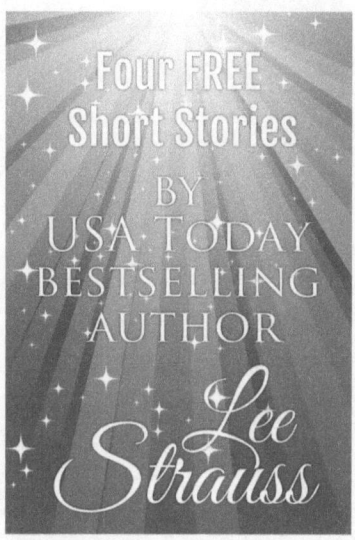

https://www.leestraussbooks.com/subscribe-four-free/

ABOUT THE AUTHOR

Lee Strauss is the bestselling author of the Ginger Gold Mysteries series and the Higgins & Hawke Mystery series (cozy historical mysteries), a Nursery Rhyme Mystery series (mystery, sci-fi, young adult), the Perception Trilogy (YA dystopian mystery), the Light & Love series (sweet romance) and young adult historical fiction. When she's not writing or reading, she likes to cycle, hike, and kayak. She loves to drink caffè lattes and red wines in exotic places, and eat dark chocolate anywhere.

Lee also writes younger YA fantasy as Elle Lee Strauss.

For more info on books by Lee Strauss and her social media links, visit leestraussbooks.com. To make sure you don't miss the next new release, be sure to sign up for her readers' list!

Did you know you can follow your favourite authors on Bookbub? If you subscribe to Bookbub — (and if you don't, why don't you? - They'll send you daily emails alerting you to sales and new releases on just the kind of books you like to read!) — follow me to make sure you don't miss the next Ginger Gold Mystery!

 follow me on
goodreads

www.leestraussbooks.com
leestraussbooks@gmail.com

BOOKS BY LEE STRAUSS

On AMAZON

Ginger Gold Mysteries (cozy 1920s historical)

Cozy. Charming. Filled with Bright Young Things. This Jazz Age murder mystery will entertain and delight you with its 1920s flair and pizzazz!

Murder on the SS *Rosa*

Murder at Hartigan House

Murder at Bray Manor

Murder at Feathers & Flair

Murder at the Mortuary

Murder at Kensington Gardens

Murder at St. Georges Church

Murder Aboard the Flying Scotsman

Murder at the Boat Club

Murder on Eaton Square

Murder by Plum Pudding

Murder on Fleet Street

Lady Gold Investigates (Ginger Gold companion short stories)

Volume 1

Volume 2

Volume 3

Higgins & Hawke Mysteries (cozy 1930s historical)

The 1930s meets Rizzoli & Isles in this friendship depression era cozy mystery series.

Death at the Tavern

Death on the Tower

Death on Hanover

A Nursery Rhyme Mystery (mystery/sci fi)

Marlow finds himself teamed up with intelligent and savvy Sage Farrell, a girl so far out of his league he feels blinded in her presence - literally - damned glasses! Together they work to find the identity of @gingerbreadman. Can they stop the killer before he strikes again?

Gingerbread Man

Life Is but a Dream

Hickory Dickory Dock

Twinkle Little Star

The Perception Trilogy (YA dystopian mystery)

Zoe Vanderveen is a GAP—a genetically altered person. She lives in the security of a walled city on prime water-front property along side other equally beautiful people with extended life spans. Her brother Liam is missing. Noah Brody, a boy on the outside, is the only one who can help ~ but can she trust him?

Perception

Volition

Contrition

Light & Love (sweet romance)

Set in the dazzling charm of Europe, follow Katja, Gabriella, Eva, Anna and Belle as they find strength, hope and love.

Sing me a Love Song

Your Love is Sweet

In Light of Us

Lying in Starlight

Playing with Matches (WW2 history/romance)

A sobering but hopeful journey about how one young Germany boy copes with the war and propaganda. Based on true events.

As Elle Lee Strauss

The Clockwise Collection (YA time travel romance)

Casey Donovan has issues: hair, height and uncontrollable trips to the 19th century! And now this ~ she's accidentally taken Nate Mackenzie, the cutest boy in the school, back in time. Awkward.

Clockwise

Clockwiser

Like Clockwork

Counter Clockwise

Clockwork Crazy

Standalones

Seaweed

Love, Tink

YOUR LOVE IS SWEET

CHAPTER 1

GABRIELE HAD DARED her to do this. "Just walk in, sign your name, and play a song for heaven's sake." It was easy for her to say. Eva Baumann's sister didn't understand what it was like to be afraid. What it was like to be invisible. Gabriele oozed confidence, tall and lithe like a runway model, lighting up every room she entered. She was pretty, talented, smart.

And not handicapped.

Eva eyed the graffiti-marred entrance of the Blue Note and watched as other musicians and-patrons strolled into the darkened room. Music pumping from the sound system escaped into the narrow corridor of four-story stone buildings every time the heavy wooden door opened and closed. Eva carefully set down her guitar case and rested her hand over her chest, willing her heartbeat to slow. The muscle pulsed erratically, and her stomach wanted to dry heave.

Eva gripped her cane with white knuckles. She'd learned to master the uneven sidewalks with careful steps, but the cobblestones were still a nemesis, especially in colder months like February. The rubber knob on the tip of her cane had to center on a stone, otherwise she could lose her balance and fall. It was necessary to wait for a break in traffic or to continue to the corner for a walk light before daring to cross the street.

She took a deep breath. She could do this. This was just an irrational fear—not real. Nothing bad would happen to her in that room. It was filled with people who loved music as much as she did. It was loud and crowded and dark, and no one would expect her to talk. When they called her name, she'd focus on the small stage, blocking out everyone in the room out until she safely stepped up. Then she'd just close her eyes and pretend she was at the street church playing to the people who came for the soup they provided.

She could do this.

A cold wind blew hair across Eva's face and she snapped to attention just as the little green man flashed on to indicate it was safe to walk. She lumbered across with a guitar in her left hand and her cane in her right. The weight of her instrument pulled her shoulders forward, her back arching slightly under her winter jacket. She caught her reflection in a store window and frowned. She looked like a crazy, old lady, not a twenty-year-old girl.

Eva tucked her cane under her left armpit and reached for the door. It swung open sharply, a patron had exited at the same moment, and she was shoved against the wall, nearly losing her balance.

"Excuse me," the guy said. He held the door open, waiting for her to go in. She wanted to turn around and head straight home, but the guy's eyes stayed on her, waiting. The cold air whooshed inside.

It would be impolite not to pass through. "Thank you," she said softly. She leaned on her cane and entered. She'd been to the Blue Note before. Gabriele and her British boyfriend Lennon Smith had dragged her out one night, so she knew what to expect. There was a bar to the right and table seating to the left. A poster on the wall read: "If you want to chat with your pals while the band is playing, take your conversation outside." The air smelled of beer and cigarette smoke clinging to damp wool jackets. At the back of the mid-sized room was a small stage lit by two lights hanging from the ceiling.

Her stomach churned, and once again she questioned herself. Why had she come? What did she have to prove? Why did she care so much what Gabriele thought? She stared back at the door.

"Hello, *ma Cherie*. Would you like to sign your name?"

The gruff yet friendly voice stopped Eva before she could leave. She knew the manager, Herr Maurice Leduc, by reputation, but had never spoken to him before. "I don't know," she answered.

"Well—" His eyes darted to the guitar in her hand. "I just thought since you lugged that thing in with you." He pushed the sign-up sheet closer.

Eva didn't have the heart to deny the man. She took the pen and scribbled her name.

"Wonderful," Herr Leduc said with a sincere grin that filled a round face. "I look forward to hearing you play..." he glanced down at his sheet, "Eva Baumann."

The room consisted of a lot of wood. Tables, chairs, benches and floors—all darkly stained, old wood. Even the ceiling had rough, open wood beams. Eva claimed a nearby empty chair and breathed in and out, long and slow. She was here. She'd done it. Wait until she told Gabriele. Wouldn't she be surprised?

A server arrived, and Eva ordered a cola. The other people who shared the long table gave her sideways glances at her childish drink and cheered each other as they lifted their beer glasses.

Herr Leduc walked on stage and welcomed everyone. He called the first act, a girl with long, golden hair, he introduced as Katja Stoltz.

Eva listened intently, impressed with the girl's talent and the way she took over the stage like she owned it. That was what Eva needed to do. Own it.

The girl finished her song, and after much-deserved applause, she joined her friends at a table across the room. A guy in his early twenties with a peacock tattoo along one arm stood to give Katja Stoltz a hug. He had messy, dark brown hair and bristles on his face, like he hadn't shaved in a few days. He laughed and high-fived her before sitting and draping the peacock around a thin girl with spiky hair.

A shiver ran up Eva's back. She recognized that guy. Last summer, when she was playing guitar for the home-less, many of them had raised their hands to God in praise.

The outside metal blinds had been raised, they always were when the church was open, and a group of guys had stopped to watch from across the street. They began to laugh and then threw their arms in the air, mocking the people worshiping inside.

That was the first time Eva had seen that peacock tattoo, and she'd never forget the laughing face of the handsome guy who went with it.

Her short-lived confidence shriveled at the thought of being the man's next target. Oh, why did she come? She'd leave right now if she thought she could do it without making a scene. The room had filled, and there was no way she could slip out unnoticed with her guitar and her cane.

She sipped her cola and kept her eyes focused on each act as it was called. Every time Herr Leduc stepped to the mic to call a name, Eva's heart filled with nervous dread and emptied with a flush of relief when she didn't hear hers.

"Sebastian Weiss," Herr Leduc said.

The guy with the peacock tattoo hooted, shifted out from behind his table and grabbed his guitar.

So that was his name.

He hopped onto the stage and strapped on a guitar with an over-confidence Eva envied. She wanted him to be terrible so that she could add self-delusion to his other obvious traits of conceit and insensitivity, but unfortunately he wasn't. His voice was smooth and strong, and he had great range.

She also happened to notice the flex in his biceps that poked out of the short sleeves of his dark T-shirt and how his jeans fit nicely on slender hips.

He finished his song and fisted the air like he just won a boxing match. The audience went crazy. Eva couldn't help but join in the applause. Something about Sebastian was electric. His aura and competence, his popularity—she couldn't peel her eyes off him. His arm returned to its position around the girl beside him who hadn't smiled once. Such a contrast to Sebastian who couldn't stop smiling. He seemed quite taken by the pixie girl and kissed her excitedly on the cheek.

"Eva Baumann."

What? Eva had been so busy watching the table of cool people, she hadn't been paying attention.

Herr Leduc's accented German bellowed again. "Eva Baumann."

Eva's heart stopped. Then raced. Her hands broke out into a sweat, and she blinked back the tears welling up behind her eyes, which were opened far too wide. Her head prickled hotly, and she swallowed hard. She could sense the attention of the room, necks craning, everyone searching, waiting for the next act to stand.

Herr Leduc stared at her, and all she could do was shake her head. He gave her a gracious nod and called the next name.

A girl with short, dark hair bounced out of her seat, and within seconds Eva was forgotten. She took advantage of the swirl of commotion that occurred between acts, grabbing her guitar and cane, and limped to the entrance.

It was a terrible mistake to come, she thought as she hobbled down the crusty street. She kept her head bowed low against the cold, and gripped her guitar case and her cane. If she'd had a third hand, she'd swipe at the bitter tear that slid down her cheek.

On Amazon

Acknowledgements

WRITING a book is like raising a child—it takes a whole village to do it. Much thanks to my "village!"

First, there's my singer-songwriter husband Norm Strauss whose idea that we should work on something together was the catalyst of this book, and my son Joel whose song "Sun & Moon" was the seed that inspired Katja and Micah's story. Also Sarah Brendel and Kim June Johnson who contributed songs that inspired ideas. Special hugs and kisses to Kim for giving Katja a musical voice.

My friends and family in BC, Canada and also in Dresden, Germany.

And as always, my Heavenly Father who gently guides and watches over me.

Song Links

Listen to all the songs featured in Sing Me a Love Song as recorded by Canadian Folk artist Kim June Johnson.

Visit the songwriters!

Sarah Brendel
Listen to Think Back written and performed by Sarah Brendel,

Norm Strauss
Listen to How Deep Can You Feel written and performed by Norm Strauss

Kim June Johnson
Listen to Don't Go Now written and performed by Kim June Johnson

Joel Strauss
Listen to Sun & Moon written and performed by Joel Strauss

Watch the music video of Sun & Moon on youtube.

Listen to all the songs from A Light & Love Sweet Romance on Bandcamp at songsfromtheminstrel.band-camp.com

ARTIST LINKS

Andrew Smith
www.andrewsmithmusic.com
Norm Strauss
www.normstrauss.com
Joel Strauss
www.joelstrauss.com
www.joelstrauss.bandcamp.com

Joshua Smith

www.joshuasmithtunes.com
www.joshuasmith.bandcamp.com

Permissions

SUN & MOON

Words and music by Joel Strauss. Copyright Joel Strauss. Remake recorded by Kim June Johnson. All rights reserved. Used by permission.

THINK BACK

Words and music by Sarah Brendel. Copyright Sarah Brendel. Remake recorded by Kim June Johnson. All rights reserved. Used by permission.

HOW DEEP CAN YOU FEEL

Words and music by Norm Strauss. Copyright Norm Strauss. Remake recorded by Kim June Johnson. All rights reserved. Used by permission.

DON'T GO NOW

Words and music by Kim June Johnson. Copyright Kim June Johnson. All rights reserved. Used by permission.